THE MISTRESS OF ROSEHAVEN

Left widowed and in debt, Rosemary Shaw has no choice but to accept an invitation from an uncle she has never met to come and live at his Rhode Island mansion, Rosehaven. But from the minute she arrives with her young children, she finds the place ominous and unsettling. Even as she begins to fall in love with the mysterious Will Hennessy, it seems that someone is prepared to go to any lengths to prevent Rosemary from becoming the new mistress of Rosehaven . . .

ROSEMARY SANSUM

THE MISTRESS OF ROSEHAVEN

Complete and Unabridged

LINFORD
Leicester

First published in Great Britain in 2017

First Linford Edition
published 2017

A catalogue record for this book is available
from the British Library.

ISBN 978–1–4448–3511–3

Published by
F. A. Thorpe (Publishing)
Anstey, Leicestershire

Set by Words & Graphics Ltd.
Anstey, Leicestershire
Printed and bound in Great Britain by
T. J. International Ltd., Padstow, Cornwall

This book is printed on acid-free paper

1

The journey from our home in Connecticut to this lonely Rhode Island mansion overlooking the storm-tossed North Atlantic had been a long one, and fatigue, mixed with sadness, was finally wearing upon us.

Even though my children, Jonathan and Frances, had still to fully understand what had happened, I knew that they felt it as well — the notion that all was not quite *right* . . . and might never be right for them again.

Barely three weeks had passed since we had buried their father — my husband, John. And now, having packed the few meager belongings we intended to take with us, we had embarked upon the long, demanding train journey to my Uncle Joseph's home.

Towns followed each other with regular monotony as the train pushed ever eastward: Cheshire, Middletown and Hartford, and then Marlborough, Bozrah and Voluntown. Great stands of timber and the occasional fast-flowing river blurred past our carriage window, and as a backdrop, there rose great timbered mountains, purpled by distance.

Then the darkness of early evening fell and we could no longer see much of anything, and with nothing to occupy them, the children tried to find relief in sleep.

For me, however, sleep was impossible. Though I wanted the rock and sway of the carriage to lull me into a doze where I would no longer have to think about the uncertainties that lay ahead of us, I couldn't. Instead, I used the time to try and convince myself that I had made the right decision.

And I had . . . hadn't I?

The main problem was that I had never known my uncle. The only thing I could really say for him was that his invitation that I come join him in neighboring Rhode Island had arrived at exactly the right time. My husband's death at the shockingly young age of thirty had left me with a number of debts. John had been a speculator, you see, and a good one. But towards the end of his life many of his investments had taken a turn for the worse, and I believe it was the worry and stress of having taken other people's money and invested it, only to then lose it on their behalf, that contributed to his heart attack.

Determined though I was to do so, I knew I should never be able to settle his debts myself. But in his letter, my uncle had assured me that, having heard of my misfortune, he would deal with everything. For the sake of my children, I had no choice but to put my faith in him, and agree to move into his home. Although I had no way to know for sure, I thought perhaps that now he was well into his old age, he wanted a companion of sorts.

I looked across the carriage at

Jonathan and Frances. Both children shared my coloring — strawberry-blond hair and large, expressive blue eyes. In sleep the pair of them looked so vulnerable, and I ached for their loss, even if they themselves weren't completely able to.

Please don't misunderstand me. John had been a wonderful man. In the beginning, he was as charming as charming could be. But his work had been his life, and I had accepted long ago that everything else had to take second place to his career. I was old enough to understand that, and I acknowledged it — albeit reluctantly. After our marriage, however, he grew even more distant than I could have imagined, as his desire to make money and be the best at what he did slowly but surely consumed him.

If I was honest with myself, my children had never really known their father. To them he had always been a remote, preoccupied man, who sometimes came into their lives but seldom stayed long, and was more often to be found working endless hours to make money for his clients.

It hurt to admit it, even to myself, but Jonathan and Frances didn't really know what it was like to lose a father, for John had never been much of a father to begin with.

As for my Uncle Joseph . . . all I knew about him was what my late mother had told me on the one single occasion we had discussed him. She said he had always been a loner, and left home at an early age to seek his fortune. In this he had been successful indeed. He had gone into the oil business at just the time when oil was first being discovered in Oklahoma, Texas and California, and made vast sums of money when a use was found for it that went beyond simple illuminating fuel. He had then invested wisely in a long list of other businesses, all of which had done well.

Mother had told me that Uncle Joseph had been quite a handsome man in his time, a man who got things done, but to the best of her knowledge he had never married, and perhaps that was just as well. I knew first-hand that a man who put commerce before all else made a poor partner, and an even poorer parent.

It was late in the evening when we finally reached our destination: a small, sea-facing village called Phoenix Port. We climbed wearily to the platform and inspected our new surroundings somewhat apprehensively. The station itself was lit only by a few lanterns that swung lazily in a cold breeze, and by their glow I saw that we were the only passengers to alight there. Behind us, the train huffed and puffed and hissed steam as if impatient to be gone from the place. There came a shrill whistle, and then the train did exactly that. Within moments it was swallowed by the darkness, and all at once I felt more isolated and alone than at any time since John had died.

But I had my children to think of. I

could not betray my misgivings to them. So, putting on a brave face, I said with an enthusiasm I did not feel, 'Come along, help me with these bags. I'm sure Uncle Joseph must be outside, waiting for us.'

We passed through the deserted station house and out into a small, hedge-enclosed yard beyond. Although the light here was even poorer than it had been on the platform, a gibbous moon showed us a four-wheeled Brougham carriage standing several yards away, with a man, heavily muffled against the wintry chill, seated upon its high seat.

Seeing us, he climbed down, his movements slow and ponderous. As he came toward us, I saw that he stood well above six feet in height. He was large and imposing, his bulk encased in a thick black overcoat, the lower half of his face hidden behind a tightly wrapped gray scarf. I had an impression of dark, intense eyes and a long beak of nose — then the brim of his black wool

Cahill hat threw shadow over even those features.

He loomed above us, and when he spoke, his voice was a deep rumble that was in no way pleasant.

'Mrs. Shaw?' he said.

I nodded, temporarily unable to find my voice. Then, 'Y-yes. I am Rosemary Shaw. Th-these are my children, Jo — '

'I am Kaylock,' he interrupted. 'I will take your bags.'

And, plucking them from us, he carried them back to the Brougham as if they were weightless.

After stowing them safely, he opened the carriage door and stood to one side in silence. Not wanting to keep him waiting, I hustled the children into the coach and then followed them inside. The coachman closed the door behind us and the carriage rocked as he used the wheel to climb back to the high seat. After a moment we heard the snap of a whip and the two-horse team broke into a trot.

The station house fell behind us and

I sat forward, trying to get a look at Phoenix Port itself. Aside from a few lamplit windows, I could make out nothing save a narrow cobbled street, and then even that vanished from sight, to be replaced by a lane hemmed in on either side by tall white pines.

I felt Frances press herself a little closer to me. At five, she was far too young to understand anything of what had happened, but old enough to know what she did and didn't like — and being stuck in this shadowy coach, headed into a dark night and an uncertain future, was certainly unsettling her.

On the other side of me, seven year-old Jonathan reached out and squeezed my hand. A lump immediately came to my throat. Seven years old, I thought, and yet his instincts were to offer me whatever comfort he could. I had always loved my children, of course, but in that moment I loved them with an intensity I had never experienced before.

'Not long now,' I said softly. 'And then we can all see our new home.'

Twenty minutes went by, and each one seemed to last far longer than it should have. Then, finally, I sensed that the carriage was slowing down, and leaned forward so that I could see our new home for the first time.

I almost wished I hadn't.

In his letter, Uncle Joseph had told that his home was called Rosehaven, and that it had been built to his own specifications. The name had sounded so safe and inviting, I had expected the house itself to offer similar comfort at just the time when the children and I needed it. But I was wrong. My first and lasting impression was that it was a forbidding place, and yet again I questioned the wisdom of having been too ready to accept Uncle Joseph's invitation to come here.

Rosehaven was an ugly gothic pile which rose to great, fussy heights, with Autumn arches and ornate stonework. As we drew closer to the place, it seemed to me that the grotesque gargoyles perched at intervals along the lip of the tiled roof watched our approach through malevolent eyes. I told myself that they were rain-gutters and no more, but the ugly little imps, with their overlarge features and sneering mouths, still presented an unsettling effect upon me.

How would the children feel when *they* saw them?

A central stone stairway led up to a large oak and steel-strapped door. To either side, the rest of the house stretched off into the darkness. How many rooms did it contain, I wondered? There was no way to tell for certain, but the place was huge — huge, and intimidating because of it.

The Brougham drew to a halt before Rosehaven, and the carriage rocked a little as Kaylock climbed down and wordlessly opened the door for us. I felt Jonathan and Frances press themselves even closer to me, and this time it was I who reached out to give each of them a reassuring squeeze. I climbed down from the carriage and hesitantly, doubtless scared by the enormous Kaylock and overawed by Rosehaven itself, they joined me and did not stray far from my skirts.

'Thank you,' I said to the big coachman. He merely turned, climbed back to the seat and gigged the horses to a walk. The Brougham vanished around the north wing of the house.

I suppressed a shiver that had nothing to do with the chill of the night, and together we walked up the steps until we reached the front door. I pulled a lever to one side of the door and somewhere inside I heard a bell jangle shrilly.

A few moments later the door swung open and a middle-aged woman stood before us: short, portly, and dressed in the black-and-white uniform of a servant.

'I am Rosemary Shaw,' I said hesitantly. My mouth was dry with nerves, and when she spoke, I was glad there was no need for me to say more.

'Yes, Mrs. Shaw,' she replied in a neutral tone. 'We've been expecting you.'

So saying, she stood aside so that we might enter.

We looked around the reception area in which we found ourselves. It looked less like a home than the foyer of some dark and dingy museum. The ceiling was high, their exposed beams lost in shadow, the walls were of dark oak, as was the floor. The furniture was old and heavy, the portraits on the walls of pale-faced, unsmiling people we had never known and never would. Lamplight threw distorted shadows in every direction.

'Come this way,' said the maid, for so I took her to be. She set off across the reception area at a brisk walk, her heels clicking and clacking and sending echoes up through the vast house.

She came to a set of double doors and rapped smartly on one of the panels. A male voice on the other side of the door said, 'Come.'

The maid opened both doors and then stepped aside to allow us entry. I felt the children grip my hands even tighter as I led them into a cheerful, well-appointed sitting room.

'Mrs. Shaw,' said the maid. 'And her children.'

A man was standing before a fireplace that was large enough to step into. The fire behind him danced and flickered around a stack of logs. The man himself looked at us for a long moment, and try as I might, I could not read his expression. His eyes, which were blue and as sharp as chips of ice, gave nothing away.

The moment stretched on. The children began to squirm, and it was all I could do to meet his gaze and not look away.

'Thank you, Alice,' he said after a moment, still not taking his eyes from me. 'That will be all.'

The servant withdrew from the sitting room and the doors clicked shut behind us.

For a moment then, the man studied us some more. He was tall and lean, perhaps sixty, and he dressed in a suit of dark broadcloth, with a deep scarlet cravat at his throat. His iron-gray hair was thick, and it curled a little over his ears and at the nape of his neck. His face was long, with a straight nose, hollow cheeks, a narrow mouth and a well-defined chin. He wore his sideburns long, so that they traced the line of his jaw.

Unable to stand the charged silence any longer, I said hesitantly, 'Uncle Joseph?'

He shook his head. 'Your uncle is away on business,' he replied. 'I am Hayden Cross, your uncle's business partner.'

I was disappointed that my uncle wasn't there to greet us, but forced a smile. 'I am very pleased to meet you, Mr. Cross,' I said politely.

His only response was a brief, sour twitch of the lips. 'I fear our acquaintance will only be a short one, Mrs.

Shaw,' he replied. 'You see, your uncle has . . . reconsidered . . . his original invitation to you — and has decided to withdraw it.'

I frowned at him, not able to comprehend exactly what he was saying. 'Excuse me?' I managed at last.

He shrugged one bony shoulder. 'Put simply, Mrs. Shaw,' he replied, 'you are no longer welcome here.'

2

I blinked several times, then said in a near-whisper, '*What?*'

Stepping away from the fireplace, Hayden Cross brushed back the folds of his black frock coat and slid his hands into his pockets. 'Your uncle made his offer in a moment of . . . weakness,' he replied. 'He is an old man now, and a recent illness confined him to bed and gave him rather too much time to contemplate his own . . . mortality. Fearing that his time was near, he convinced himself that he should do something to make amends with his family — of whom you, Mrs. Shaw, are the sole survivor — and, hearing of your recent widowhood, wrote his impetuous letter, suggesting you come and stay with him.'

'*Live* with him,' I corrected absently.

He inclined his head. 'As you wish.

But then Joseph recovered; and, if anything, is healthier now than before he fell ill, and more active than ever. That being the case, he realized that he had been somewhat premature in considering himself finished, and has thrown himself back into our business endeavors with renewed vigor. Thus, with so many new responsibilities to occupy him, he felt that he could no longer honor his invitation. His prolonged absences, travelling the country for months at a time in order to oversee our many subsidiaries, would hardly be fair on you and your . . . ' He hesitated. ' . . . children.'

'I still don't understand,' I said doggedly. 'I — we — came all this way on his say-so. We gave up *everything* to come here!'

'I'm sure you did,' he agreed smoothly. 'But if we are honest, Mrs. Shaw — you did not have *much* to give up.'

I opened my mouth to argue that point, but instead said nothing. After all, he was *right*. What *had* we given up to come here? A comfortable house, yes; but one upon which the bank would be certain to foreclose now that we had fallen upon hard times: one that now held only memories of what had been, and what could and should so easily have been instead. That was all.

Still —

'I have certain . . . obligations,' I said, and my voice broke a little as I said it. 'My uncle told me he would help me meet them.'

Cross nodded. 'So I believe. But you must understand, dear lady, he was not in his right mind when he wrote to you.'

'Then . . . ' I groped for words, but couldn't seem to find any.

'We will, of course, attend to your comfort tonight. That is the least we can do. But tomorrow, it would be as well for you to return where you came from.'

The pronouncement struck me like a blow. Of all the things that might have awaited us at the end of our journey, I had not foreseen this as being one of them. I wondered how anyone could be so cruel as to change their mind in such a way; but again, I reminded myself that I did not know my uncle and could not have anticipated his change of heart.

I felt beaten down. Truly, this was the final straw. I had fallen into a largely loveless marriage and tried to make the best of it. I had worked hard to be both mother *and* father to my children, when John had been otherwise engaged for so much of their formative years. I had become a widow whilst still in my middle twenties, and left with debts I could never realistically hope to settle.

Enough was enough.

In the circumstances, I saw no option but to thank this man, Hayden Cross, for telling me news that must have been embarrassing in the extreme for him, and that we would indeed go back to Connecticut in the morning . . . though what we would do when we got there, and how we would survive, remained to be seen.

I opened my mouth to say as much, and that was when I felt the children pressing against the folds of my mourning-black taffeta dress, one on either side of me.

They had trusted me to bring them to a new and happier life, and I had failed them. But, almost at once, I corrected myself. I had acted in good faith: it was their *Uncle Joseph* who had failed them.

For myself, I cared naught. But my children had been let down by a man who had chosen to enter our lives unbidden with promises of hearth and home and, yes, salvation. And all at once I felt an anger rise within me that was wholly out of character.

'I will, if I may, stay until my uncle returns from his business trip,' I said stiffly.

Hayden Cross looked surprised. 'I'm afraid — '

'With respect, Mr. Cross,' I interrupted, 'you are my uncle's business partner. I am his relative by *blood*. The least he owes me, after fetching my children and I all this way under what amounts to false pretenses, is to tell me to my face that I am not wanted here.'

His thin features tightened. 'Now, see here — ' he began angrily, and it was all I could do to stand my ground and not back down.

'I did not ask my uncle for help,' I reminded him. 'It was *he* who reached out to *me*. Until I received his letter, I had not even thought of him since I was a girl. As hard as it is to understand, I accept that he changed his mind. That was his prerogative. But I do *not* accept that he should foist the duty of telling me as much upon someone else!' My emotions were a maelstrom inside me. Tears threatened to blur my vision, but I would not give in to them.

'I think you forget yourself, madam,' he said coolly.

'Not at all.' My eyes dropped to his

hand. 'I see that you are married, Mr. Cross. How would your wife feel if — '

'Don't bring my wife into this!' he said with a vehemence that startled me. 'You did not know her, and cannot presume to know how she would have behaved in any given set of circumstances!'

I realized from the way he had referred to her that he was a widower, and instantly regretted my mistake. 'I apologize,' I said softly. 'But the fact remains, Mr. Cross, that we will either prevail upon your hospitality and stay here until my uncle returns, or we will find lodgings somewhere in the village. But I will not return to Connecticut until my uncle has looked me in the eye and seen what a disappointment he has been to me!'

Cross's mouth narrowed still further, and I could see that he was beside himself with anger. Somehow he bit back whatever he had been about to say, and took his hands from his pockets. They clenched and unclenched rapidly, I noticed.

'I had hoped we could be . . . amicable . . . about this unfortunate business,' he said. 'I see now that we cannot. However, I cannot grant your request. Your uncle will be away for several weeks yet. You cannot possible prevail upon our hospitality, as you call it, for that long. You have your children to consider — they need a stable environment, schooling, and to be among children of their own age. They will have none of these things if you insist upon staying here or in Phoenix Port.'

'Nevertheless,' I said, 'that is what I intend to do. My uncle owes me — us — an explanation and an apology in person, and I intend to see that we receive it.'

'Madam, you are sorely trying my patience,' he said. 'But I can understand your . . . chagrin. And for that reason, and from my own pocket, I will send you back to Connecticut with enough money to settle your husband's debts, and enable you to live — frugally, I admit — in reasonable comfort until you find a way to support yourself.'

'I do not want your charity, Mr. Cross.'

'Mrs. Shaw — ' He stopped, perhaps seeing from my expression that my mind was made up. Silence filled the sitting room for a long moment, broken only by the crackle of flames as they danced in the hearth. Then: 'It has been a long day for you, I am sure, and you must be tired. I suggest you rest tonight and we will discuss the matter again on the morrow.'

'I will not change my mind,' I warned him.

'Nevertheless,' he persisted, 'you may see things in a different light tomorrow.'

Without waiting for another response, he went to a long silk sash that hung to one side of the fireplace and tugged at it. A few moments later there came a discreet knocking at the door, and he said, again, 'Come.'

Alice entered the room. 'Yes, Mr. Cross?' she asked deferentially.

'Take Mrs. Shaw and her children to the Green Suite, if you will. And have Kaylock deliver her luggage at once.'

'Yes, sir.'

He turned his back on us then, and made a pretense of warming his hands at the fire. I knew we had been dismissed with the gesture, and we turned away and followed the maid from the room.

Inside I was trembling, but as much now with fear as with anger. Although my fear was for our future, which seemed more uncertain than ever, I did not regret the stance I had taken. I felt that the very least Uncle Joseph owed us was an apology in person. For all I knew, he hired and fired his workers with little thought for their personal circumstances. If that was indeed the case, then I wanted him to understand that every action had a consequence . . . and that the consequence was not always pretty.

Alice led us to a wide staircase and, taking the children's hands in mine, we began to ascend behind her. Our footsteps echoed up to the vaulted ceiling, but nothing else in the great house stirred. Around us, all was dark and gloomy, lit only by ornate wall lanterns that threw out precious little light. As we reached the first-floor landing, I consoled myself with the thought that perhaps it was just as well that we would not be living in such oppressive surroundings after all.

We followed Alice along a corridor until we reached a door halfway along the left-side wall. She opened it and went inside, leaving us to wait on the threshold until she found and lit a lamp. The light chased away shadows and revealed to us a large, comfortably furnished room. I saw at once why it was called the Green Suite — the walls were papered with a heavy flock paper, pale green as a background, upon which had been overlaid a series of raised vines and roses in a darker, emerald green.

We entered, and I inspected the suite more closely. The main room contained a large double bed, a heavy wardrobe in dark oak, a dressing table, a chest of drawers and a writing bureau. French windows directly in front of me opened out onto a narrow balcony and the dark night beyond. At one end of the room stood an empty fireplace. At the other, a door opened onto a separate bedroom, which contained two single beds.

'Will that be all, ma'am?' asked Alice, once she had finished lighting two more lamps.

I nodded. 'Yes. Thank you.'

She left the room without another word, closing the door softly behind her.

At last I allowed myself a heartfelt sigh of relief. Until that moment, I hadn't realized how tense I was, how rigid I had been holding myself. As I unbuttoned my travelling coat, I sensed the children watching me. Forcing a smile, I bent and saw to their comfort, helping each to take off their outer coats.

'Are we really going back to Connecticut?' asked Frances.

'Yes,' I replied. 'Eventually.'

'Is it because Uncle Joseph doesn't want us here?' asked Jonathan.

'He's busy right now,' I told him. 'You heard what Mr. Cross said.'

'I don't like Mr. Cross,' Jonathan decided.

'Neither do I,' said Frances, pouting.

'That's very rude,' I told them. 'In any case, I doubt we will be seeing much of Mr. Cross after tomorrow.'

'Good,' said Jonathan, decisively. 'I don't like it here.'

'Well, we're not staying for long,' I assured him. 'Now — '

There came a brisk rapping at the door. I crossed the fussy Tabriz carpet to answer it.

Kaylock was standing outside, our luggage in his massive hands. He had removed his coat and muffler to reveal a face that was heavy-featured, with a heavy brow and a broad lantern jaw. Wordlessly, he brushed past me and deposited our cases in the center of the floor. Then he turned and left the room.

I closed the door behind him. The man had an unsettling effect, and I had to force a smile back to my face as I returned to the children.

'Come along,' I said as brightly as I could manage. 'Let's find your night-clothes and — '

Frances looked up at me very seriously. 'Can we sleep with you tonight, mummy?'

Just then, I would have had it no other way. 'Of course you can.'

She seemed to brighten a little at that. But then Jonathan drew my attention to another matter.

'I'm hungry,' he said.

I realized then that we had been shown the bare minimum of hospitality. There had been no offers of a hot drink to ward off the chill of the night, or a snack of some kind; Alice had not even bothered to light a fire in the room, and neither was there fuel with which I might hope to set one myself. It came to me that then we were being treated just like the poor relations we were, and that only made me all the more determined to stay here, or in the village, until my uncle came home. No one was going to treat my family in such a cavalier manner.

'Come on,' I said. 'It's been a long day and I'm sure you're just as weary as I am. Let's change into our nightclothes and snuggle up together.'

And that was how we came to spend that first night together in the double bed, cuddled up to each other for warmth and comfort, and hoping that, in sleep, we would forget all about how hungry we all were.

3

Sleep eluded me for much of the night, as I had expected it would. But I must have drifted off eventually, because the next time I opened my eyes, sunlight was streaming in through the French windows. A new and hopefully better day had dawned, I told myself . . . but I knew there would be another confrontation with Hayden Cross before we left this place, and I did not relish it.

I eased out of bed so as not to disturb the children, and quickly saw to my ablutions. I chose a black dress to signify mourning, but suddenly changed my mind. This place was dreary enough as it was, and I felt we needed brighter colors to lift our spirits. So I defied convention and dressed instead in my favorite two-piece navy blue calico day suit, with puffed sleeves and a white undersleeve.

At last I felt ready to face the new day. By then the children were awake, and with a promise that today would be much better than yesterday, I urged them to wash and dress.

At last we left the Green Suite and descended the wide staircase, followed by the eyes of the austere figures in the paintings that lined the walls. A tomb-like silence hung over the house. Even our footsteps, as we made our way to the ground floor, seemed strangely muted.

As we reached the foyer, we saw Alice crossing the cold black-and-white checkerboard floor. She heard us and turned, but there was no smile of greeting on her countenance, just the studied indifference of the servant.

'Good morning Mrs. Shaw,' she said. 'I expect you will want breakfast before you leave us.'

Anger flickered within me at her insolence, but all I said was, 'Indeed.'

'Come this way,' she replied. 'I will show you to the dining room.'

She led us past the sitting room in which we had first encountered Hayden Cross, and opened the next set of double doors she came to. A long refectory table, upon which sat a variety of covered silver serving dishes, dominated the room. The smells of eggs, bacon, deviled kidneys, tea, coffee, freshly-squeezed orange juice and more, stirred the hunger in us.

Mr. Cross was seated at the head of the table, buttering a freshly baked roll with an expensive silver knife. He looked up as the doors opened, and setting the knife aside, rose to his feet.

'Good morning, Mrs. Shaw,' he said with the slightest tilt of his head. 'I trust you and your . . . children . . . slept comfortably?'

'Thank you, yes,' I replied, a little stiffly.

He indicated that we should take places at the table, then sat and continued to butter the roll. We took our seats, but as hungry as we were, we did not attempt to take and fill plates until he said, 'Please — help your-selves.'

The selection of food, all of it piping hot and appetizing, was quite amazing. I had never seen such variety. But I made sure our portions were modest. Perhaps foolishly, I did not want to be in this man's debt any more than I could help.

'I very much regret that we got off on the wrong foot yesterday,' he said, but his tone was perfunctory: he was saying the words, not especially meaning them. 'I hope this morning we can settle our differences more amicably.'

'I wish we could,' I replied. 'But my mind is made up, Mr. Cross.'

'May I ask you a question, madam?'

'Of course.'

'What difference does it make if you receive your apology from Joseph or from me?' he asked. 'For years now, I have spoken on Joseph's behalf. My word has always been good enough before this.'

'And I would not wish to suggest

otherwise,' I replied. 'But it is a matter of principle. Had he made some effort to stop us before we left everything behind us, perhaps I could have forgiven him. But to let us come all this way, and then learn that he has left to pursue his business interests elsewhere, leaving — forgive me — a stranger to tell us we are no longer wanted here — '

'I sympathize entirely, dear lady,' he interrupted. 'To a point. But I think you are missing the wider picture.'

'Which is . . . ?'

'That there has, by your own admission, already been enough disruption in your life. Staying here, threatening to find lodgings in the village, until you can look your uncle in the eye and tell him what a terrible person he is . . . Well, may I speak frankly?' Without waiting for a reply, he went on, 'You do yourself and your children a grave disservice, Mrs. Shaw. I believe you are a better person than that.' He sat forward a little. 'Your children need a stable environment in which to grieve for the loss of their father. To delay that by one or two months, however long Joseph will be away, just because *you* decide you want an apology in person . . . well, I believe you owe your children more than that.'

'Mr. Cross, I assure you that the welfare of my children is my prime concern. I intend to find lodgings in Phoenix Port and put them into school there until my uncle returns home. They will want for nothing during that period. Once I have spoken with my uncle, we will leave and never return.'

'Then your mind really is made up?'

'It is.'

'Very good, Mrs. Shaw.' Cross pushed his plate away from him, his appetite apparently gone. 'But there will be no need to find lodgings elsewhere. Joseph would never forgive me if I allowed you to stay anywhere but here until he comes home.'

I wasn't entirely sure how to feel

about that. I wanted to leave this place, and so did the children. But, though I had said I would find lodgings in the village, I knew that would cost more than I could comfortably afford to spend, our financial circumstances being what they were.

Besides, I wanted to give Hayden Cross the benefit of the doubt. Perhaps he was trying to offer the hand of friendship that had been so sorely missing the night before. If that was indeed the case, then it would be churlish to refuse him.

'Thank you,' I said. 'We will not outstay our welcome, Mr. Cross. We will only stay until my business with Uncle Joseph is concluded.'

Apparently satisfied by my assurance, he rose and left the room, closing the door softly behind him.

Jonathan stopped eating and, looking up at me, said gloomily, 'Does that mean we're staying here after all?'

'Only for a little while,' I replied. 'Now, eat up, the pair of you. Then we can explore the grounds.'

★ ★ ★

We wore coats against the cold wind and went out into the grounds. I looked back at the house, believing it would look better in the sunlight, but I was wrong. With its odd angles and dismal gray stone walls, it looked somehow malignant. I tried to tell myself that it was just my imagination running away with me, but somehow I couldn't believe that.

We went around the house, our footsteps crackling on the gravel. The wind smelled of the sea — salty, briny, and of something wild and untamed. When we stopped to admire the gardens laid out behind the mansion, we could hear the *shushing* of waves in the distance, throwing themselves against the rocks.

We explored numerous game trails and what the children called secret paths, watched insects buzzing and fluttering, and chuckled at the capering of some playful squirrels as they chased each other up and across the boles of misshapen trees. The grounds were surrounded by thick woods, and the forest floor — what I could see of it — was dim with the shadows of a million interlaced branches. The trees themselves looked to me to be peculiarly *crooked*, as if something had happened during their growth to stunt and misshape them. I shivered at the thought, and found myself wondering yet again whether or not I was allowing my imagination to run away with me.

After a few moments, I found an explanation for the strangeness of the trees. They had grown up in the wind coming off the sea, and *that* had dictated the pronounced lean they all seemed to share. I felt better then, because I had dispelled some of the eerie feeling that the house had inspired within me.

My relief, however, was short-lived. As we followed a bend in the path, we came in sight of a small, ivy-covered gardener's shed. In itself, it was quite beautiful. But standing before it, cleaning a set of shears, stood Kaylock.

Even though some thirty feet separated us, he heard us coming and slowly turned to look at us. The eyes beneath his heavy brow were cool and enigmatic, and much as I wanted to offer him a smile and a friendly nod, I couldn't. Just the very sight of him, so massive, so emotionally distant, made me anxious to escape his presence. The children obviously felt the same way, for they tugged on my hands, wanting to leave this part of the grounds as soon as possible.

One by one, Kaylock stared at us all in turn. It was impossible to know what he must be thinking. Without taking his eyes off us, he suddenly snapped the shears shut, and I flinched at the sound. He saw that, and something that might have been a smile made his mouth quirk a little.

He did it again.

Snap!

And then, to my alarm, he then started to approach us.

There was something almost hypnotic in his gaze: it seemed to sap my will to turn and leave. Each step he took brought him closer and closer, and he punctuated every other one with another vicious snapping of the shears.

Snap! Snap! Snap!

Every time the sun glinted off the blades of the shears I flinched again.

And then —

Without warning, there came a sudden snapping as of a branch in the trees to our left. Kaylock stopped in his tracks, and turned ponderously in that direction. He stood there for a long time, staring into the shadows of the close-growing trees, but when I followed his gaze, I could see no one — the woods appeared empty.

While he was still distracted, I turned, and we hurried back around the bend in the path until the storage shed was out of sight. Even then, I kept us walking so quickly that it was all Jonathan and Frances could do to keep up with me. Constantly I looked back over my shoulder, but after a time it became clear that Kaylock did not intend to pursue us.

I slowed a little then. I had no idea what had been in the giant's mind as he approached us, but if the look on his face was anything to go by, it was nothing good. But what did he have against us? Or perhaps Hayden Cross was behind his strange behavior. Did my uncle's business partner want to make us so unwelcome here that we would be glad to return to Connecticut?

Again I tried to convince myself that my overwrought imagination was playing tricks on me. Perhaps — probably — it had.

But I promised myself I would never go anywhere near that storage shed ever again.

★ ★ ★

I was just reaching out to open the door to the Green Suite when I heard a soft sound from within. Not knowing what to expect, I had to steel myself for a moment before I opened the door and peered inside.

A maid, whom I had not previously met, was standing on a small stepladder as she used a feather duster to flick down the green flock wallpaper. She turned as she heard the door open, and immediately descended the ladder in order to offer me a curtsy.

'Mrs. Shaw?' she asked. She was about eighteen, I judged; of average height, with slightly waved brown hair brushed to the back of the head, where it was caught up in short curls and bound with a very heavy plait. Her face was plain but pleasant, her build chubby.

I nodded cautiously. 'Can I help you?'

'I'm Jane, ma'am,' she introduced. 'Mr. Cross gave me instructions to come up and clean your suite.'

I glanced around. As near as I could see, everything was exactly as I had left it, and the room itself was spotless.

'Thank you,' I said. 'You've done a very good job.'

She looked at me strangely. 'I haven't *started* yet, ma'am. I've only just arrived.'

'Well . . . as you can see, there's no need to clean the room today. I'm sure you have other duties to attend to.'

Jane shook her head. 'I had better do it, ma'am,' she insisted. 'Mr. Cross said he wanted the place spotless, and that I was to dust every wall and polish every flat surface. He was very clear about it.'

Had I been mistaken about Uncle Joseph's business partner, then? Was he trying to make up for the ill feeling that had developed between us?

'I can come back later, if you'd prefer,' she offered. 'But I *have* to do it.'

'Very well,' I said, and then, as the idea occurred to me, 'We'll help you, won't we, children?'

Jane's gray eyes went round. 'Oh, I

couldn't allow that, Mrs. Shaw.'

'Why not?'

'Well . . . it's not right. I'm paid to do this sort of work. You . . . well, you're the lady of the house.'

I laughed when she said that, and realized that I hadn't laughed in a long, long time. 'Is that what Mr. Cross called me?'

'No, ma'am, I . . . well, I don't know what else to call you.'

'Well, I'm a visitor, nothing more, and certainly no one special. Now, shall we get to work?' When she continued to hesitate I said, 'I won't say anything to Mr. Cross, if that's what's worrying you. It will be our secret.'

She relaxed then. 'It doesn't seem right,' she said. 'But if you're set on it, ma'am . . . '

'I am.'

Jane had fetched a scuffed, wooden-handled box with her that was stuffed with little tins of wax polish and bright yellow dusters. I handed Jonathan and Frances a duster each and sent them off to their room with instructions to wipe every surface clean. I knew they would soon give up on such a mundane chore, but I wanted to keep their little minds occupied as much as I could.

'Do you really need to dust the wallpaper?' I asked Jane as she climbed the stepladder and began to use the feather duster again.

'Yes, ma'am. Mr. Cross was very particular about that. Apparently these flock wallpapers harbor quite a bit of dust if they're not cleaned regularly.'

I waited until Jane had finished the section she was working on, then began to dust the furniture nearby. There was no doubt that Jane had dislodged more dust that I would have expected from the wallpaper.

We worked in silence for a few moments, and then I asked if Phoenix Port had a school.

'Yes, ma'am,' came the reply. 'A small one, but a very good one. I was educated there myself.'

'Will they take my children on a

temporary basis, do you think?' I asked. 'For a month or so, I mean?'

Jane glanced over her shoulder at me and smiled. 'I should think Miss Twickenham would be delighted to, ma'am.'

'Miss Twickenham?'

'She runs the school, a dear, sweet spinster lady . . . and I swear she never met a child she didn't like or couldn't win over.'

At last, I thought, *some good news* . . . though I wasn't sure the children would see it that way.

4

That evening, supper was what I later learned was a local specialty — what they called a boiled dinner in that region. All cooked together in one pot, it was a delicious blend of corned beef, cabbage, carrots, turnips and potatoes. To my surprise, the children, who had always been fussy eaters, set to with relish, and left clean plates behind them.

Halfway through the meal I broke the uncomfortable silence between us by asking Hayden Cross if I might go into Phoenix Port the following morning. He didn't reply immediately, just looked at me through those ice-chip eyes of his, from his seat at the head of the long table. In the distance there came a low rumble: a storm sweeping in off the sea, I thought.

'I want to enroll Jonathan and

Frances in school,' I explained.

He considered that for a moment longer, then said, 'I will have Kaylock drive you in first thing tomorrow morning.'

Kaylock. I almost shuddered just at the mention of his name. I had wanted to avoid that man as much as possible, but now I realized that would not be quite so easy, since there was no other way to get into the village unless he drove us in the Brougham.

Again there came a low growl of thunder.

'Will that be acceptable?' Cross asked when I made no immediate reply.

I nodded. 'Yes. Thank you.'

As soon as he had finished his meal, he stood up, accorded me a stiff nod, and left the room without another word. The atmosphere in the dining room was still heavy, and I knew I had been mistaken when I thought he had sent Jane up to clean the room as a way to build bridges between us.

There was nothing else for us to do

in that large, ugly house as the sun went down, so I decided that an early night would do us all good. Tired out from the active day I had arranged for them, the children offered no argument.

As we climbed the stairs to the accompaniment of our own lonely footsteps, the staircase was illuminated by a sudden flare of lightning. Frances grabbed at my skirts and I reached down to pick her up.

'Silly,' chided Jonathan. 'It's only a storm.'

'But it frightens me,' she protested.

'Everyone knows the clouds are only knocking their heads together and laughing about it,' he reminded her with absolute seriousness.

'It's true,' I fibbed. 'Anyway, we're safe and sound here, in the house.'

But to my surprise, I found myself wondering just how safe we really were. There was no reason why we shouldn't be, of course . . . and yet remembering the look on Kaylock's face that morning, the way he had tormented us by constantly snapping the shears between his enormous hands . . .

I dismissed the notion. I couldn't afford to think that way, not right now. Instead, I brought to mind a poem I had learned many years before, and whispered it gently as I carried Frances the rest of the way up to the Green Suite.

'*When the boughs of the garden hang heavy with rain, And the blackbird reneweth his song, And the thunder departing yet rolleth again, I remember the ending of wrong.*'

I was pleased to see that, in our absence, someone had built and lit a fire in the hearth. I suspected it had been Jane. After all, she was the only one who had shown us anything like friendship since we arrived. The fire cheered us up and sent shadows dancing across the flock wallpaper.

I lit the lamps and helped the children prepare for bed. They wanted to sleep with me again, and in the circumstances I didn't have the heart to refuse them. Soon they were tucked in, and after a while both were soundly asleep.

I was about to prepare myself for bed when I realized that I had been so distracted I had not yet closed the drapes. As I went to do just that, I thought I saw something beyond the French windows, out in the darkening grounds below — a movement, perhaps, within the trees that hemmed the gardens.

It might have been my imagination, but I didn't think so. Quickly, I brushed aside the lace, opened the doors and stepped out onto the narrow balcony.

At once the chill of the evening struck me and raised gooseflesh on my arms. I stood there for a moment, looking down over the grounds. Clouds scudded across the starry sky, creating shadows where none had existed mere seconds before, and in the distance I heard waves battering the coast. I felt the first gentle patter of the coming rain —

And then —

A great sheet of white lightning flared across the sky . . . and I saw a man, bundled up against the inclement weather, lurking in the treeline!

My intake of breath was a sharp sound.

This had been no trick of clouds moving across the moon — I had *seen* him — I *had!* At once I leaned forward to get a better look at him, but all I managed was the briefest glimpse of . . . what? A shadow, quickly retreating back into the darkness of the woods.

Who was he, I wondered, and why had he been there? I realized that he had been standing in a spot that would afford him an excellent view of our suite, and again my thoughts turned to Kaylock.

And yet . . .

And yet Kaylock was monstrous in size. The man I believed I had seen down there — a man who might still be watching me from the shadows even now! — was of more average size.

Hayden Cross, then? Was it *him?* Who else could it be? Who else had any right to be on my uncle's property? And why was he watching our suite from hiding?

I waited a moment longer, staring into the shadowy timber, hoping for a better look at him. I was rewarded only by the distant yapping of a coyote. Then there came another surly growl of thunder, the pattering of the rain grew more insistent, and I went back inside, locked the doors and pulled the drapes closed behind me.

Was it too late, I wondered, to change my mind and take the children to live in the village until Uncle Joseph came home? Or should I just forget about Uncle Joseph altogether and leave this wretched place once and for all?

My heart was racing, and the shock of seeing . . . *someone* . . . watching our suite from the woods had left me dry-mouthed. I went to the chest of drawers and poured myself a glass of water from the carafe there. I drank, then grimaced, for the water had a curious metallic taste to it.

Again I looked at the drapes, closed now against the wild night. *Yes*, I thought. *We're safe inside the house.*

But, that night, I was careful to lock the door to the Green Suite before I went to bed.

★   ★   ★

The storm moved further inland sometime after midnight, and when I woke the following morning it was to another bright and sunny day. No amount of sunshine could brighten the mood of the children, however.

'Do we have to go to school?' asked Jonathan.

'Yes, you do.'

'Can't we stay with you?'

'You need an education,' I explained as I got them washed and dressed.

Jonathan pulled a face. 'Can't *you* teach us?'

'No, I can't — certainly not as good as a real teacher can.'

'I don't want to go to school,' whined Frances.

'I don't know why, I'm sure,' I replied. 'Think of all the new things you'll learn, and all the new friends you'll make.'

'We don't need friends,' said Jonathan. 'Anyway, my tummy hurts.'

Fondly, I ruffled his hair. 'Oh, no, young man. I'm not falling for *that* trick! After breakfast, we're going down to the village and enrolling you in the school — no arguments! Remember what Jane said yesterday? She said the school is run by a very nice lady named Miss Twickenham. I'm sure she'll make sure you settle in quickly and learn all kinds of wonderful things.'

'Will you stay with us?' asked Frances.

'I don't think that would be allowed,' I told her. 'But I will meet you after school and . . . and we'll all have tea somewhere!'

They brightened at the prospect.

After breakfast, I found Alice in the

kitchen and asked her to have Kaylock fetch the Brougham around to the front of the house. She stopped what she had been doing — making butter in a barrel churn — and stared at me in her usual surly manner.

'Mr. Cross said he would take us into the village this morning,' I explained.

The maid straightened up and wiped her hands down her white apron. 'Very well,' she said, clearly unhappy about it. 'But it looks as if this batch of butter will be ruined. It's supposed to be churned constantly, you know.'

It was open disrespect, of course, but I didn't want to make a scene about it. 'Then the sooner you find Kaylock, the sooner you can continue churning,' I replied coolly.

She stared at me for a moment longer, no warmth in her whatsoever, then let herself out through the back door and vanished along the garden path.

I released a breath. I had no idea why she disliked me so. Perhaps she had been told I was here to somehow take advantage of my Uncle Joseph, and was protective of him, as so many servants were of their employers. In that case, I could hardly blame her for her attitude — the woman clearly knew no better. Still, there was no doubt that it made things more awkward and unpleasant for me than they needed to be.

Upstairs in our suite, the children had grudgingly donned their coats for the journey into Phoenix Port. I forced a bright smile as I took my own gray frock coat from the wardrobe and buttoned it up, but with the prospect of school before them, neither Jonathan nor Frances was in the mood to smile back.

When we left the house, the Brougham was waiting for us at the foot of the stone steps. Kaylock, muffled against the chilly day, sat on the high seat, whip in hand. I looked up at him and offered a smile, but he ignored it. I realized that he wasn't even going to climb down to open the

Brougham door for us, and so did it myself. The children climbed inside and I followed them, and even before I had closed the door behind me, I heard the crack of his whip and the carriage lurched into motion.

As I fell back against the seat, Frances said, 'That man scares me.'

'Me too,' said Jonathan.

'Hush, now,' I told them. 'Let's just enjoy the ride.'

As the carriage followed a narrow, winding road away from the house, I felt my own troubled mood begin to ease. It was as if a pall of gloom hovered over Rosehaven and affected all who dwelt beneath it. Leaving the house behind was almost like casting off shackles and being free again.

The sunshine, together with the beautiful Rhode Island countryside, helped. Vibrant green hedgerows and tall trees gave way to vast fields laid out in patchwork shapes, the fields shelving away toward low, forested hills resplendent with the colors of the fall

— oranges and reds, yellows, magentas and pinks. I looked up at a sky so blue that it almost hurt just to see it, smudged here and there with lazily drifting clouds. Black ducks scooted up from a wind-ruffled pond as we passed, while ruby-throated humming-birds hovered above flowers so they could feast on their nectar. Once we saw a magnificent stag watching us from the middle of a field. Then the scene was replaced by a tobacco field that seemed to go on forever.

At length the village came into sight, and Kaylock brought the carriage to a halt outside the schoolhouse. It was a quaint little building set in a neat garden surrounded by wildflowers, and I felt that the children would soon grow to like it there, for it was so different to our more sinister surroundings back at the house.

Kaylock made no move to climb down and open the door for us, so once again I did so for myself and helped the children climb down. Jonathan and

Frances looked up at me with distinctly unhappy expressions, doubtless trying to convince me that I was being unbelievably cruel by expecting them to attend school.

'I have no idea how long this will take,' I called up to Kaylock.

'Well, I can't wait,' he replied, his voice a low rumble. 'I have other duties to perform, you know.'

'Yes, I know, but — '

'You'll have to find some other way of getting back,' he growled. And before I could say more, he snapped the whip above the heads of his two-horse team and turned the Brougham around. We watched in silence as the carriage headed back the way it had come, and Jonathan reached up and took my hand in his.

'We don't want to go back to that house anyway, do we?' he said.

I smiled down at him. 'Let's not worry about how we're going to get back just now,' I replied. Then, taking them both by the hand, I led them through a white picket gate and up a narrow path toward the schoolhouse door.

Miss Twickenham was a short, matronly woman in her late fifties, with fine fair hair and a ruddy complexion. Hers was a face to which smiles came easily, and though she was unquestionably eccentric, she was also possessed of boundless energy and a friendly manner which soon won the children over.

'Indeed, indeed, we can always find extra places for children such as these!' she said, after I had introduced us and asked if any places were available. 'How do you do, young Master Jonathan? And Miss Frances! My, what a pretty dress you're wearing! Why don't you two go into the classroom and have a look around? When the other children arrive, I'll introduce you. It won't take long to make new friends, I'm sure!'

As Jonathan and Frances went into the classroom, Miss Twickenham continued confidentially, 'I am so sorry for your recent loss, Mrs. Shaw. I will keep an eye on the children for you while they are here, and if I see anything I believe you should know about, rest assured I will let you know. But frankly, I think a school environment will be the best thing for them right now. It will keep their little minds busy, and I'm sure they will quickly settle in.'

'I hope so,' I replied. 'Routine is what they need just now.'

'Well, we certainly do stick to our routines here. But if you have any concerns, please do not hesitate to raise them. School begins at nine and ends at three-thirty. I will tell them that you will meet them from school at the appropriate time.'

'Thank you,' I said. 'I know they will be in good hands.'

* * *

Outside, I turned my collar up against the stiff breeze that was coming in off the sea, and wondered how I could arrange transportation for the journey home. There must be someone in Phoenix Port who would run the children to and from school every weekday, and though it would eat into my meager savings to employ him, employ him I must, if the children were to receive their education. I decided that I would make enquiries while I was here.

It quickly became obvious to me that Phoenix Port was a place of great beauty. The picturesque main street was made up several different business establishments, some, like the U.S. Post Office, built from red brick, but most of whitewashed clapboard. I walked past the railroad depot where Kaylock had first met us, and spotted the spire of a church pointed skyward behind what appeared to be a large factory at the village's farthest end.

The hour was still early, and those few people out and about were hurrying to their jobs. I decided to sightsee for a time and then return to the Post Office. If anyone knew of a coachman for hire, I thought it would be the local postmaster.

In the meantime, I crossed the road and followed a narrow path through a stand of birch trees that swayed and rustled in the salty air. At length I found myself on a grassy headland overlooking the ocean. It was quite the most beautiful spot I had ever seen. A gentle breeze blew across the turquoise water, creating a million, million white-top waves, and on the horizon I spied the flapping sails of a stately packet ship. Some miles from the packet, another ship slid across the horizon, gray against the blue sky, its funnel leaving a black smudge of smoke in its wake as it plowed on toward the south.

I halted a short distance from the edge of the cliff and looked up at the wheeling gulls, plovers and pelicans, envying them their freedom. The coastline itself was equally stunning, dominated as it was by long tracts of sand interspersed with grassy dunes, and the white column of a lighthouse some miles away, beside which sat a little, red-roofed cottage.

And then, hardly more than a half-mile offshore, the ocean's surface suddenly broke, and a whale, oily black with white markings, sprang up into the air, dripping spray like molten silver, before crashing back into the depths. It was a sight that truly took my breath away.

For a moment then I forgot all my troubles and drank in the wonderful sights, sounds and smells around me.

. . . *around me* . . .

I realized then that I was feeling light-headed, that my thoughts were racing and tumbling over each other. Again I looked out to sea, but this time the horizon had tilted drunkenly and I felt unsteady on my feet.

Without warning, my legs suddenly seemed unable to support me, and I knew that I was going to faint. Dimly I realized that I had drawn closer to the jagged edge of the cliff than I should have — that I was going to tip forward over the precipice and that would be my end.

I thought of Jonathan and Frances, and I thought I whispered their names, but could not be sure.

Then everything blurred and I fell forward — to my doom.

5

I pitched forward — and then stopped
abruptly as someone grabbed me from
behind and checked my headlong fall.
As his fingers tightened around my
upper arms I heard him say gently,
'Hey, hey . . . it's all right. I've got you.'
And then I felt him drawing me back
from the edge of the cliff.

Perhaps it was the sudden, over-
whelming sense of relief I felt, but I *did*
faint then, for I remembered no more
until I opened my eyes and found
myself in his arms as he carried me
slowly and effortlessly back through the
birches toward the main street.

Still disorientated, I began to panic
and he stopped, gave me a reassuring
squeeze and said again, 'It's all right.
You're all right, now.'

I stopped struggling and looked up
into the face of a man I had never seen

before. He was tall and broad-shouldered, about twenty-eight or so, with an appealing and somehow trustworthy ruggedness to him. His thick hair was blue-black. It curled slightly at the ends and fell in a spill across his forehead. Well-spaced eyes as green as the leaves on a fir tree regarded me concernedly from beneath arched brows. His nose was straight, and overhung a broad mouth that was serious now. His skin was the color of an old penny, which told me that he spent much of his time outdoors. He had a strong, square jaw, pitted with a dimple, and he dressed functionally in white shirt, open at the throat, a long, burgundy-colored sack jacket and black-wool trousers tucked into knee-high boots.

'I — '

'You fainted,' he said, his voice a gentle baritone. 'Fortunately I was there to catch you.'

I remembered it all then, and said, 'I . . . I'm all right, now. I don't know what came over me . . . '

He studied me for a moment longer, making sure I really had recovered. Then he said, 'Will you be all right if I set you down?'

I blushed, realizing that I was still in his arms. 'Yes! Yes, I — '

Carefully he set me down on my feet, held me for a moment longer until he was sure I could stand unaided.

'How do you feel?' he asked.

'Better.'

'Well, you still look a little pale to me. Come on, let's get you out of this chilly wind. There's a teashop in the main street. You'll feel better when you have something hot to drink.'

I held back. 'I'm sorry . . . I don't — '

He smiled and held out his right hand. 'Forgive me, we haven't been introduced yet. My name is Hennessey. Will Hennessey.'

'Rosemary,' I said, still a little distracted by what had happened. 'Rosemary Shaw.'

71

I took his hand and it felt comfortingly warm against my own cold one.

'I'm pleased to know you, Rosemary Shaw,' he said pleasantly, and glanced in the direction of the street. 'Shall we?'

My thoughts still a little jumbled, I was happy to let him take charge. Down in the harbor, men were rolling heavy barrels down off a moored three-master. Idly I asked my companion if the barrels were bound for any of the inns and taverns we had passed, and he laughed.

'I would hope not, Mrs. Shaw,' he replied. 'They contain whale oil, not wines or spirits!' He gestured to the factory I had noticed earlier, at the far end of the main street. 'That's where the whale oil is bound for. They turn it into candles, and sell them all over the eastern states.'

A few moments later, we entered the olde-worlde teashop he had mentioned, and when we were seated at a window table, he ordered tea and some pastries. In the hearth, a fire was licking at a pile of chopped logs, and the warmth made me feel better.

'I can't imagine why I fainted like that,' I said. 'I've never fainted in my life.'

'Perhaps the bereavement took more out of you than you realized,' he suggested.

I looked at him sharply, immediately on my guard. 'How did you know I had recently suffered a bereavement?'

'Your sleeve,' he said, indicating the black band I had placed on my left sleeve as a sign of respect for John.

I had forgotten it was there, and forcing myself to relax again, said, 'Perhaps. It has certainly been a trying time. Anyway, thank you. You've been most kind.'

He dismissed the idea with a gesture, and poured tea. 'Do you live in these parts, Mrs. Shaw?'

'N-no. That is, I thought I might live here, but . . . '

'You changed your mind?'

I nodded, adding, 'Well, had it

changed for me, really.'

'Oh?'

This time it was my turn to make a dismissive gesture. 'Please, pay me no mind. I . . . well, it's been a difficult time, just recently, and this morning I placed my children in the local school and . . .'

'You miss them?' he guessed with an understanding smile.

'I do. But I know that school is where they should be just now.'

'How many children do you have?'

'Two. Jonathan is seven, and Frances is five.'

'May I assume, then, that it was your husband who passed away?'

Not trusting myself to speak, I could only nod.

'And you came here thinking to start a new life?'

Again I studied him closer. 'Exactly. But . . . well, let's say I made a mistake. As soon as I can, I intend to return to Connecticut.'

'But not for a while?'

'No. I have . . . a certain matter I need to take care of before we go back.'

'I see.'

'You don't,' I told him. 'You couldn't possibly see.'

'Well, then let's say I . . . understand.'

The tea was every bit as reviving as he had said it would be. 'Have you lived here long?' I asked.

'I don't live here at all,' he replied. 'I'm staying at the Mason Hotel.'

'You're a visitor, then,' I said. 'As well as a Good Samaritan.'

He chuckled. 'Well, I'm not sure about that, but . . . yes, I'm just visiting.'

'May I ask what brings you here?'

He hesitated for a moment, then said, 'I've always fancied myself as a writer. I thought I might write a history of Phoenix Port and came to have a look around and do some research.'

'Then I'm stopping you from your work,' I said.

'Not at all. Indeed, you have provided a very welcome distraction.'

'Do I assume from that, that the history of the village isn't as interesting as you first thought?'

'All history can be somewhat . . . dry, unless you can find a way to bring it to life. The only really dramatic or exciting thing about Phoenix Port is its name.'

'Oh? Why is that?'

'There was a bad fire here, back in the summer of 1797. It started in the textile mill at the other end of town and a blustery wind coming in off the sea ensured that it spread fast. Men, women, even some of the older children, they all did what they could to contain it, but to no avail. By dawn all that remained of the village was smoldering embers and lost memories.'

'I can see that you're a writer,' I said.

He smiled self-consciously. 'Well, that was it. The village was finished. But then the mayor recalled the legend of the phoenix.'

'Which is . . . ?'

'According to Greek mythology, the phoenix was a long-lived bird that renewed itself every five hundred years.'

'I remember now!' I said. 'It dies in a fire and . . . is reborn from its own ashes!'

'Precisely,' he said, and quoted Dante: ''*Even thus by the great sages 'tis confessed, The phoenix dies, and then is born again, When it approaches its five-hundredth year.*''

'So instead of leaving, the townsfolk built a new village out of the ashes of the old one.'

'Yes.'

'Well, that sounds pretty exciting to me.'

'It is,' he agreed. 'And it will make an exciting chapter in my book . . . but I'm afraid everything else will seem rather tame by comparison.' He picked up his cup and blew steam off its contents. 'Where are *you* staying, might I ask?'

'Rosehaven,' I said, and I thought his expression changed minutely when I said the name, though I couldn't be sure. 'Do you know it?' I prompted.

He nodded. 'Oh, yes. I know it, all

right. Is it that you have decided not to live there after all?'

'I was promised a place there by an uncle. But he changed his mind.'

'Did he, indeed? Did he tell you why?'

'He hasn't told me a single thing,' I said. 'He is away on business, and left it to his partner.'

'And yet you are still there — and plan to be there for quite a while, apparently, since you have enrolled your children in the local school.'

I suddenly felt very foolish. 'It was silly, really. I . . . I felt the very least my uncle could do was tell me to my face. So I elected to stay until he returned home.'

'And when will that be?'

'I don't know. Mr. Cross was rather vague about — '

'Mr. Cross?'

'My uncle's business partner.'

He nodded. 'Of course. I'm sorry, please go on.'

'Well, there really isn't much left to

say. I said I would stay at Rosehaven or here, in the village, until he returned home and Mr. Cross said I could stay there.'

'But you don't like it there?'

'No,' I said wretchedly. 'But I have my pride. I won't let him chase me away.'

'And is that what he's been trying to do?'

I deflated. 'I don't know,' I confessed miserably. 'It has been such a wretched time, I can hardly think clearly as it is. All I know is that my children and I have been made to feel anything *but* welcome there.'

'Perhaps you *should* leave, then.'

'Perhaps I should,' I agreed. 'But it's as I said. I have my pride.'

'*Proverbs*, verse eighteen,' he murmured.

'I'm sorry?'

''Pride goes before destruction',' he quoted. 'Sometimes it's better just to cut your losses.'

I didn't like the sound of that much.

To change the subject, I said, 'Are you a religious man, then, Mr. Hennessey?'

He laughed at that. 'I'm afraid not, ma'am.'

'And yet you quote the Bible.'

'I have an enquiring mind, is all. I pick up little facts here and there and somehow they just . . . stick.'

'Such as . . . ?'

He thought for a moment, then said, 'Well . . . all the swans in England belong to the queen. If you drop a raisin into a glass of champagne, it will bounce up and down continuously. A banana isn't really a fruit, it's a herb. Need I go on?'

I couldn't help laughing. 'Now you're just teasing me.'

He raised his right hand, palm out. 'They're all true, I swear. I am a collector of information, sometimes useless, sometimes not — but always, I hope, entertaining.' He set his cup down. 'Well, it's nice to hear you laugh, Mrs. Shaw. And I must say, you're looking much better.'

'I *feel* better,' I confessed. 'But I'm afraid I can't stay much longer. I have business to which I must attend.'

'Anything I can help you with?'

'You've already been of more help than you know,' I replied. 'No — I need to arrange a carriage to take my children to and from school.'

'Didn't this fellow Cross arrange that for you?'

'He arranged for his . . . manservant, gardener, I'm not entirely sure what he is, really . . . to fetch us here today. Then I was told I would have to make my own arrangements from now on, and he returned to Rosehaven.'

'Well, I wouldn't concern yourself too much, Mrs. Shaw,' he said. 'I'd be happy to provide such a service for you.'

I was taken aback by his unexpected offer, and shook my head. 'Oh, I couldn't. You've already done enough — '

'I insist,' he said. 'And frankly, you'd be doing me a favor, giving me something to do other than scratch around Phoenix Port, looking for a scintillating history that doesn't exist!'

'But you would have to ferry the children to and from school five days a week!' I protested.

'That's no hardship. I *like* children. I used to be one myself!'

I laughed again.

'Look,' he said, 'the owner of the Mason Hotel has an old Cabriolet Phaeton — I've seen it in the barn behind the hotel. He never uses it, and I'm sure he'd be only too happy to rent it out to me.'

'Then I shall pay whatever he asks — '

He grinned at me. 'There's that pride again.'

'Is pride such a bad thing?'

'No. But sometimes it can be . . . misplaced. Please, Mrs. Shaw, I would consider it a privilege to help you.'

There was something in the way he said it, something about the way he looked at me . . . he was so earnest, so sincere, so . . .

I found myself blushing, for I had no right to consider him as warm and handsome as I did. Such thoughts were inappropriate for a woman who had been so recently widowed.

'That's settled, then,' he said in good humor, even though we had really settled no such thing. 'When will you require my services, ma'am?'

'Are you sure about this, Mr. Hennessey?'

'I would have it no other way, Mrs. Shaw.'

'Well, the children leave school at three-thirty. I promised I would be there to meet them, and I said I would take them to tea before we return to Rosehaven.'

'Then I will meet you here at, say, four-thirty?'

'Better still,' I suggested impulsively, 'why don't you join us? You've been so kind, it's the least I can do.'

He considered that, then nodded. 'Thank you. Shall I meet you here at about three-thirty, then?'

'Yes.'

'I look forward to it,' he said. 'But now, I fear I must take my leave. I have some . . . research I need to conduct.'

'Of course. The last thing I want to do is keep you from your work.'

He rose and took my hand in his. 'Until later,' he said.

And I simply could not help myself — I could hardly wait until I saw him again.

★　★　★

I spent the remainder of the day sightseeing and thinking back over my meeting with Will Hennessey. He had come along at exactly the right time, when I needed a friend the most. Just to have spent even a brief time in the company of someone who was so willing to listen, commiscrate and offer help, did much to restore my flagging spirits. As for my fainting spell . . . I hardly gave it another thought. I felt perfectly fine for the remainder of the day.

At half-past three exactly, Miss Twickenham's pupils, about fifteen in number, came racing out of the schoolhouse and down the path to meet their waiting parents. When Jonathan and Frances saw me, their eyes lit up. They threw themselves at me, hugging me around the waist, and each one fought the other to be the first to tell me what they had learned that day, and all the new friends they had made.

I was so happy that they had settled so quickly into their new environment. That, at least, was something that no longer need worry me. I saw Miss Twickenham standing at the school-house door. She smiled at me and waved, and I waved back.

'Are we still going to have tea together?' asked Jonathan.

'Yes, we are,' I replied. 'And I have arranged for a very nice man to take you back and forth to school every day.'

I expected frowns of disapproval at that, but they had enjoyed their first school day so much that it appeared they couldn't wait to come back again.

Hand in hand, we walked along the main street until I saw a black Phaeton with a single horse in its traces, parked outside the teashop. A thrill went through me, for Mr. Hennessey had once again been as good as his word, and had not let me down.

We went inside and found him waiting for us at the same window table we had occupied earlier. He stood up and held out chairs for us all, ordered a cream tea and insisted that we all call him Will. For their part, the children were a bit reserved upon first meeting him, but it didn't take him long to win them over.

'Now,' he said to them when our order had arrived, 'it is very important just how we eat these delightful scones.' And he helped himself to a knife, plate and a still-warm scone to demonstrate. As Jonathan and Frances watched, clearly fascinated, he went on, 'We must carefully slice the scone in two, like

. . . so. Now, what do you suppose we do next?'

'We eat them,' said Jonathan.

'We put jam on them!' said Frances.

'No, no, no,' he replied. 'What we do is spread clotted cream over both halves.'

I watched the children watching him. They were entranced.

'There,' he said at length. 'And *now* we add the jam. But not just *any* jam — it *must* be strawberry.'

He suited his actions to his words, and had soon built two halves of a very handsome-looking scone.

'Half each, to begin with,' he said, and passed the plate across to the children. They each took a half and began eating with relish.

'Is that really the way we are supposed to serve them . . . Will?' I asked.

He nodded. 'That's the way they prefer it in a place called Devon, in England, where the cream tea originates.'

I shook my head. 'You really do know some odd facts, don't you?'

'Of course, you could try the Cornish method, instead,' he replied. 'But for that we would need to replace the scone with some sweet white bread.'

I was gratified when the children quickly began to include him in their conversation, and solicit his opinion on some of the things they had learned that day. The time fairly flew past. But then I realized that, as wonderful as the day had been for all of us, we still had to return to the house, and at once my good mood soured. I had allowed myself to forget my troubles, if only for a while, and now reality had come crashing back in with a vengeance.

It must have shown on my face, for Will asked, with genuine concern, 'Are you all right, Mrs. Shaw?'

'Please,' I said. 'Rosemary.'

He nodded. '*Are* you all right?'

I forced a smile. 'Of course.'

But he was far from convinced, and guessing the reason for the sudden deterioration in my mood, he said, 'Time to go back?'

I said, 'Yes. Time to go back.'

6

As we stepped out into the main street, Jonathan said, 'Can we ride up on the seat with Will?'

'No,' I replied. 'For one thing, I'm sure that Will has more than enough to do, just driving the coach, without having to watch you, too.'

But Will only laughed, and it was a rich, easy sound. 'They'll be no trouble,' he assured me. 'Unless you'd prefer them to ride inside with you . . . ?'

'No, no,' I replied.

With his customary good humor, he lifted first Frances, then Jonathan, onto the driver's seat, and then held the door open for me to climb inside. A few moments later I heard the snap of a whip cracking above the horse's head, and then we were on our way.

As Phoenix Port fell behind us, I listened to the children chattering to

Will, and laughing every time he said something funny. It occurred to me then that John had never paid them as much attention, and as if learning so from an early age, neither Jonathan nor Frances had approached him unless he had first given them permission. Perhaps they had secretly been afraid of annoying him, or that in his distracted state he might reject them.

Work, after all, had been John's life. Ironically, he had worked himself to death in order to support the very family from whom he had distanced himself so much. There had been few times indeed when the four of us had all spent time together, and even when we had, the children had been quiet and withdrawn, as if not entirely sure of him.

There in the relative privacy of the coach, I heard Will start singing a merry song that was popular at the time, and the children quickly joined in. With a sudden flash of insight, I understood just how devoid of love and unity we had been all these years.

'Casey would waltz with a
    strawberry-blonde,
'And the band played on.
'He'd glide 'cross the floor with
    the girl he adored,
'And the band played on.
'But his brain was so loaded it
    nearly exploded;
'The poor girl would shake with
    alarm.
'He'd ne'er leave the girl with the
    strawberry curls,
And the band played on!'

It was with a start that I realized I was crying — crying because my children had deserved so much more from their father, and because they had found it, perhaps too late, in this man whom they had known for barely an hour.

Will had been right, I thought. Pride *does* come before destruction. Had I swallowed my pride and returned to Connecticut, I would never have met

Will at all, and seen by comparison John's many shortcomings. I would have gone on believing that my marriage had been a good one, when in truth it had been little more than a hollow sham.

But already we were approaching Rosehaven, and quickly I dried my eyes and did what I could to compose myself. When the Phaeton finally pulled up before the house, I was once again in control of my emotions . . . though for how long, I really couldn't say.

The coach swayed as Will hopped down, and one by one the children, giggling, threw themselves into his waiting arms. He caught them easily, swung them around and then settled them lightly on the gravel.

'I'll be here to collect you at eight-thirty tomorrow morning,' he told them. 'Is that all right?'

'Yes!' cried Jonathan, and Frances clapped her hands in excitement.

At last he opened the coach door and helped me out.

'You certainly have a way with children,' I remarked.

He grinned at me. 'I told you. I — '

'Yes — you used to be one yourself.'

We both smiled at each other, and entirely without warning, the moment suddenly grew very serious as we looked into each other's eyes.

'What have we *here?*'

We turned at the sound of Hayden Cross's voice. He was standing in the now-open front door, regarding us through those cool, ice-chip eyes of his. Slowly he came forward and descended the steps. He regarded Will for a long moment, then turned his attention to me.

'This is a very cozy scene, I must say,' he remarked.

I squared my shoulders. 'This is Mr. Will Hennessey,' I replied stiffly. 'From now on he will be taking the children to and from school.'

Cross's thin mouth twitched a little. 'So he is a coachman,' he said. 'But a rather . . . *familiar* one, wouldn't you say?'

'You would be ... Mr. Cross, I assume?' said Will.

'I am he,' replied Cross, pompously.

'Well, Mr. Cross, I am not so much a coachman as a friend.'

'A very *fast* friend, apparently,' said Cross. 'How long have you known Mrs. Shaw?'

'Is that any of your business?'

'While she lives under my roof,' Cross replied, 'it is *indeed* my business. I should not care to see anyone taking advantage of a woman so recently widowed.'

Will smiled, but the smile did not reach his eyes. 'Oh, I'm sure you wouldn't,' he replied.

'What is that supposed to imply?'

'That I don't care for your tone, Mr. Cross, any more than I care for your insinuations,' said Will. 'Now, Mrs. Shaw and I have come to an agreement which is satisfactory to both of us. The reason we struck our bargain was because you did not see fit to have your man ... a Mr. Kaylock, I believe ...

run these children to and from school each day.'

'If that is indeed your agreement with Mrs. Shaw, I see no reason why you should be quite so . . . familiar with her.'

'I think you will find that it is called simple friendship,' said Will.

'Well, your services are no longer required, Mr. Hennessey,' said Cross. 'I will make arrangements for the transportation of Mrs. Shaw's children from now on.'

'That is Mrs. Shaw's decision to make,' said Will. 'She hired me. It is only she who can fire me — not you, Mr. Cross.' He turned to me. 'Well, Mrs. Shaw?' he asked.

I hesitated. I did not wish to antagonize Cross any more than I could help. But Will was my friend — my only friend, save for the tenuous relationship I had already built with Jane — and I was not prepared to give him up lightly. And yet . . . I did not wish to make things awkward for him. I had the sense that Hayden Cross could be a powerful enemy, if he so chose. Then again, there was something about Will that suggested he could be an equally powerful adversary.

'I . . . ' My voice betrayed me. Trying again, I said, 'I am happy with our arrangement as it stands, Mr. Hennessey.'

He nodded. 'Then I will collect the children tomorrow morning at eight,' he said.

'You will do no such thing,' hissed Cross. 'You will never return here again.'

Will turned so as to face him directly. 'I will be here at eight in the morning, as I will be here at eight every weekday morning from now on. I see little that you can do to stop me, Mr. Cross. Of course . . . ' he fell silent for a short moment, as if an idea had just occurred to him, ' . . . you could always report me to the constable in Phoenix Port. Claim that I am trespassing.'

Cross's mouth narrowed angrily.

'Or better still,' Will added, 'why not send Mr. *Kaylock* down to report the matter for you?'

At that seemingly innocent remark, Cross flinched as if he had been struck. Indeed, I thought that the anger he had only just managed to contain thus far would boil over, and that he would lash out himself. Instead he turned stiffly toward me and said in a choked voice, 'Very good, Mrs. Shaw. But whilst in the company of this man, I would thank you to remember that your husband has not been dead for more than a month!'

'That is something about which I do not need reminding,' I said vehemently, and felt my eyes begin to sting. 'Mr. Hennessey ... thank you for your continued support. We will see you tomorrow morning.'

Will inclined his head a little, then returned his attention to Cross. 'Good day to you, Mr. Cross,' he said. 'I am sure we will see each other again.'

Then he climbed back onto the Phaeton and drove the coach away.

We went directly up to the Green Suite. When we went inside, I saw immediately that Jane had been dusting again — a fine patina of the stuff lay across almost every surface. I shook my head and helped the children out of their coats.

'My tummy hurts again,' Jonathan said, and I remembered he had made a similar complaint that same morning.

'Too many scones,' I said. But he looked so forlorn that I had to take him seriously. 'Where does it hurt?'

'Here.' He indicated a spot just below his ribs.

'Bad?'

'It aches,' he said.

I felt his forehead. He didn't feel feverish at all.

'You'll feel better after a little lay down,' I decided.

Both of them were worn out after their long day, and I pulled a coverlet up over them and sat with them until they both fell asleep. Then, getting up carefully, so as not to disturb them, I wandered across to the French windows and stepped out onto the balcony. Rosehaven was a strange place, and even the brightest of days could do little to dispel the air of menace that also lodged here. Now, in the late afternoon sunshine, the woods seemed no less sinister. But at least now I could see more clearly the spot from which the mystery man I had seen the night before had been watching us. He could not have picked a better position to see directly into the Green Suite.

Too tired just then to consider the identity of our unknown watcher, I turned my thoughts to Will. When I remembered how he had taken my hand and helped me into the coach, I felt a peculiar fluttering in my tummy ... and though I tried to deny it, I couldn't — it was excitement I had felt, because ...

I was reluctant to finish the thought, but finish it I did. I was excited because the attention he had shown me had reminded me that I was a woman, and a young one at that. I had loved John — *still* loved him — very deeply. But he had not been the most demonstrative of partners. Now that I thought about it, I could not remember a single time when he had looked at me as if seeing me as the woman I was, with love or even simply with appreciation. I was there; it was as simple as that. He had seen no value in a compliment or a gentle touch. To him, such displays of affection were for the foolish and the naive.

I had often longed to catch him watching me with the love-light shining in his eyes. I had longed so often to see his mouth quirk in a secret smile that said, *I am so lucky to have you*. But never had he shown me anything other than the most perfunctory of treatment. He was mine, I was his, we had a family and until things went wrong, we had money and thus he had shown himself to be a good provider. But for anything deeper than that . . . well, he had not been that kind of man.

The way Will had looked at me, by contrast, the way he had taken my hand so gently . . . Of course, I told myself he was being polite and no more, that I knew practically nothing about him and that but for a chance meeting we would never have crossed paths at all. But I sensed that he was a good man and a sincere one, and as much as I hated to admit it even to myself, I knew I was attracted to these qualities . . . and to him.

There was a brisk rapping at the door. I stepped back into the room and answered it. Alice was standing there, wearing her usual sneer of disapproval.

'Mr. Cross would like to see you,' she said.

I glanced at the children. They were still sleeping soundly.

'I shall be down directly,' I told her.

I could imagine what he wanted to see me about. He would remind me that, as a widow, I had no right to entertain other men. And I felt a quick stab of shame, because he was absolutely right. But I had hardly done that. Will and I were friends, no more. And nothing was ever likely to come of it, for our paths would diverge once my business here was concluded.

The thought left me curiously depressed.

With some apprehension, I left the room and went downstairs. Hayden Cross was waiting for me in the sitting room, standing beside the fireplace, as was his custom.

'Who was that man?' he asked when I entered.

'You mean Mr. Hennessey?' I replied. 'I met him in the village today. He was very kind to me.'

'Was he, indeed?'

'I was taken ill. Fortunately he came to my aid before the matter could become any worse.'

'Ill?' he prodded.

'I almost fainted. Actually, I *did* faint.'

'How very convenient that he happened to be on hand.'

'I consider myself to be fortunate that he *was*.'

He drew a breath. 'Who is this man, anyway? Do you know?'

'He is a writer. He's here doing research for a book.'

'Then he is not a local man?'

'No.'

'Where *does* he come from?'

'I . . . don't know.'

'Precisely,' he snapped. 'You know next to nothing about him, madam, except what he has told you . . . and yet you have entrusted your children to his care and, frankly, you yourself appear to be entirely too friendly with him.'

'Might I ask how you reached that conclusion?'

Ignoring that, he said, 'It is not the sort of behavior I would expect from a responsible parent, and it is most assuredly not the sort of behavior I would expect from a woman who has so recently experienced the loss of her husband.'

I drew myself up. 'Mr. Cross,' I said firmly, 'that is the second time you have questioned my integrity. I hope it will be the last. I have in no way behaved improperly, and resent the implication that I have. I am, I think, a good judge of character, and have no cause to doubt Mr. Hennessey. In the time I have known him he has behaved in a most gentlemanly fashion, and is obviously of a kind and generous nature. Furthermore, my children like him, and I have come to trust their instincts where grown-ups are concerned.'

'Then you care nothing for the gossip that your relationship will excite?'

'Mr. Hennessey and I do not *have* a relationship. We have a friendship.'

'A friendship with a man you barely know,' he mused. 'Interesting.'

'I hope you are not calling me a liar, Mr. Cross.'

The smile that touched his narrow

mouth was mirthless. 'I just find it curious that you should happen across such a 'friend' upon your first trip into Phoenix Port. Are you sure you did not know him back in Connecticut?'

This time, the implication was clear.

'Mr. Cross,' I said, my voice low and shaky, 'if it were not for the fact that I have tried all my life to behave as a lady, I would take great delight in slapping you for the suggestion that I have a follower. Now, I have answered your questions honestly and to the best of my ability. Whether you believe me or not is entirely your affair.'

I turned and opened the sitting room doors. Outside, Alice flinched, for she had not been expecting me to make my exit quite so soon, and it was obvious to me that she had been listening at the doors, even though she made a vague pretense of dusting a nearby table.

'Alice,' I said.

She looked at me, and this time there was a little fear in her expression, for we both knew what she had been up to.

'Yes'm?' she said uncertainly.

'Neither the children nor I will require dinner tonight,' I said.

And without another word, I returned to the Green Suite.

* * *

Not knowing what else to do in that vast mausoleum of a house, I prepared for bed and carefully climbed in beside Jonathan and Frances. For a long time I just lay there, watching the sun go down and the sky turn from blue to gray and finally to ebony. I wondered how my circumstances could have changed so much, and so quickly. One minute, my life had been orderly and settled. The next . . .

As much as the idea of swallowing my pride and returning to Connecticut now appealed to me, it would not be fair on the children to take them out of a school into which I had just placed them. Neither did I relish the thought of never seeing Will again.

But Cross had been right. What did I really know about him? For all I knew, he might be happily married with children of his own! That would certainly explain why he had taken so readily to my two, and they to him.

In any case, why was I even entertaining thoughts of love and romance to begin with? I had no right to do so, and no real cause. Except . . .

Except for the way Will had looked at me when he had helped me from the coach. What had I seen in his eyes? To me it had been warmth, acceptance, even a hint of surprise that he should feel that way about someone he had just met.

I am sure that he had seen as much in my eyes, too.

But this was no time to entertain wild flights of fancy, of hearts and flowers and living the happy-ever-after life of the fairy tale. Our lives just now were in turmoil, and I was at a loss as to how I might rectify the situation.

I closed my eyes and tried to sleep,

but sleep eluded me. I tried for an hour, perhaps longer, then got up. My throat was dry and I padded across the room to the swish of my embroidered nightgown. I poured water from the carafe and took a sip, only to grimace at the liquid's metallic taste.

Knowing I could drink no more, I took the carafe and decided to fill it afresh. The only place I could do that was in the kitchen.

Making sure that Jonathan and Frances were still sleeping soundly, I left the room and made my way downstairs. Around me, Rosehaven was silent, but it seemed to me to be a brooding silence, like the calm before a storm. In an attempt to lighten my mood, I told myself that Will was not the only writer — that perhaps I should be one as well, with my propensity for such dramatic turns of phrase.

I reached the bottom of the stairs. The lamps had all been extinguished, but a bar of light still showed at the bottom of the sitting room doors. Not wishing to disturb Cross, or have another encounter with him, I turned toward a door on the opposite side of the foyer which led to the kitchen.

It was then that I caught a snatch of conversation from the sitting room.

' . . . I still don't like it. Who is he, and where did he come from?'

I recognized Cross's voice immediately, and was about to move on when another, deeper voice rumbled, 'Does it matter?'

That was Kaylock.

Now I stopped, for what little I had heard of their conversation intrigued me. If listening at doors was good enough for Alice, then I decided it was most assuredly good enough for me.

As I crept closer, I heard Cross say, ' . . . wish I knew. But one thing is certain — we didn't allow for this.'

There was a long pause then.

'So what do you want me to do?' asked Kaylock.

'Find out everything you can about this man Hennessey,' said Cross. 'But be careful about it. We don't want to tip our hand.'

A tingle washed through me and tightened the skin of my face. What did all this mean? Why was Will of such concern to either of these men? What was it Cross had not allowed for? And what did he mean by not wishing to tip his hand?

What was he up to?

For the first time I began to suspect that there was more going on here at Rosehaven than I had realized. But before I could really think about what I had learned ... I heard Kaylock approaching the sitting room doors.

A moment later, one of the doorknobs twisted, and he came outside into the foyer.

7

For valuable seconds I could ill afford, I stood frozen with fear. Then, finally, I stepped back from the door and quickly pressed myself into a shadowed alcove, still clutching the carafe I had been intending to refill.

No sooner had I done so than the door opened and lamplight spilled out of the sitting room to illuminate the checkerboard floor. Kaylock's hulking shadow followed it outside. Hardly daring to breath, I watched the giant close the door behind him and then lumber across to the front door, muttering under his breath the whole time. He got about halfway and then, suddenly, he stopped.

I tried to press myself even deeper into the alcove.

Ponderously, Kaylock turned and looked around the foyer. He didn't know I was there — at least I don't *believe* he did — but some instinct in him told him that something was amiss. I watched, unblinking, as he swept the darkened foyer once again with those expressionless eyes of his.

I thought, *Please don't let him see me. Dear God, please don't let him find me here.*

He took a step back into the center of the foyer. I felt sure he must see me now, but as fortune would have it, he didn't even glance in my direction. He peered up the stairs into the shadows above, and continued to stand there, listening to the darkness, for what seemed like an eternity.

Around us, the house was now silent. All that could be heard was the low rasp of his breathing. I prayed for him to turn and leave, but still he stood there, sensing that something was wrong, but not knowing what.

And then, to my horror, I realized that I was going to cough.

My throat, which had been dry to

start with, and made drier still by the fear I was now experiencing, was going to betray me. I tried to suppress the urge to clear it, for to do so would lead him straight to me.

Still he lingered.

I can't do this, I thought, still struggling not to cough. *I can't fight this much longer.*

I knew then that he *would* see me.

I felt the pulse of blood pumping in my ears, felt the butterflies in my stomach multiply and make me tremble. I clung to the carafe with hands made sticky with fear . . .

But after another second he grunted, then turned back to the front door and let himself out.

As soon as the door closed behind him I slumped and let my breath out in a rush, then cleared my throat as softly as I could behind one hand. My heart was hammering against my ribs, and I felt faint. I waited until my senses had stopped swimming, and when I was satisfied that he would not be returning, left the safety of the alcove and hurried back upstairs.

I slept hardly at all that night.

* * *

It was as well that I didn't sleep, really, for Frances woke up shortly after midnight and she too complained of an aching tummy. I rocked her gently until she fell back to sleep, and then closed my eyes and managed to doze lightly. When morning came, both the children seemed fine, but I had a terrible headache and did not feel well at all.

Somehow I managed to get them ready for school. They ate breakfast, but I simply could not face food. Promptly at eight-thirty, Will drove the Phaeton up to the house and climbed down to lift Jonathan and Frances up to the seat. He looked as happy to see them as they were to see him, but when he looked at me, an expression of concern crossed his face.

'Rosemary — are you all right?'

'I'm just a little tired, that's all,' I replied.

'Are you sure? You look just how you did yesterday, when you fainted.'

I made a vague gesture with one hand. 'I'll be all right. I'll probably try to sleep a little during the day.'

'Should I send for a doctor?' he asked.

'I'll be fine. Really. It's probably something that's going around. Both the children had tummy aches last night.'

'Well . . . all right,' he said, but he was clearly worried for me. 'Take it easy, and we'll see how you are later on.'

I wanted to tell him about the events of the previous evening — of Hayden Cross's interest in him, and his orders to Kaylock to find out everything he could about Will. But before I could summon the energy to speak, he consulted a pocket watch. 'I had better get the children to school,' he said. 'I don't want to get them there late on my first day in the job.'

I smiled briefly and watched as the coach rattled away, bound for Phoenix Port. Then I turned and went back into the house.

Although I had tried to make light of how I felt, it was all I could do to climb the stairs to the Green Suite. There, I slept for perhaps an hour or so, until I was awoken by a gentle tapping at the door. Sitting up, I called, 'Come in.'

The door opened and Jane looked in. 'Oh! I hope I'm not inconveniencing you, ma'am?'

I shook my head. 'No. But . . . don't tell me you're here to clean the room again?'

I saw then that she was carrying her wooden-handled box filled with dusters and little tins of polish, which meant that she was.

'Mr. Cross is very particular about it,' she said. 'But then, I used to have a friend whose mother was exactly the same. Hated dust, she did. I don't believe I ever saw her when she wasn't cleaning or polishing something or other. I expect Mr. Cross is the same.'

'I expect he is. I really don't know an awful lot about him.'

Jane took out her feather duster and began working on the walls. 'You surprise me, ma'am. You being a guest here ... I would have thought you knew Mr. Cross well.'

'I only met him a few days ago. Tell me, what do you know about him?'

'Next to nothing, ma'am. I only started work here myself a couple of weeks ago.'

'What about Kaylock?'

She stopped dusting and looked at me. 'That man,' she said seriously, 'scares me. Perhaps I shouldn't speak out of turn, but there's something about him ... something about him that's not quite *right*.' Suddenly she eyed me frowningly. 'Are you all right, ma'am? You look a little pale, if you don't mind me saying so.'

'I do feel a little under the weather,' I admitted.

'Then I *am* inconveniencing you.'

'Not at all. But I think perhaps I'll go for a walk, get some fresh air. The atmosphere in here is rather oppressive.'

'Very good, ma'am.'

While she continued with her chores, I went to the wardrobe and took out my coat. A few minutes later I left the house behind me, and walking slowly down to the lane and crossing it, eventually found myself following a path through dense woods comprised mostly of red maple and scarlet oak. The trees looked resplendent in their fall colors, and they lifted my mood a little. I had made the right decision to get some fresh air.

Eventually the trees thinned and the path led me through a winding corridor of bushes and shrubs until at length I reached a cliff overlooking the sea. As with the day before, I found the scene before me inspiring. The breeze carried the distant chug-chug-chug of a steamer to me, and I watched it for a while, seeing shapes in the smoke that belched from her twin stacks. I thought about the children, hoped they would have no recurrence of their tummy upsets, and again tried to puzzle out the strange conversation I had over-heard the night before, between Cross and Kaylock.

Invigorated by the sea air, I went a little closer to the edge of the cliff, and cautiously peered over. I wished at once that I hadn't. There was a sheer drop of at least a hundred and fifty feet to a series of jagged purple rocks below, between which the sea flowed and rushed in a constant white spray. It made me nauseous just to look down upon such a sight, and I quickly reversed until I was surrounded on all sides by good, firm earth.

After a while, I felt the sea breeze chilling me, and turning, made my way back to the house.

My spirits lifted again when, turning onto the gravel drive that led to Rosehaven, I recognized the Phaeton parked out front, and saw Will standing at the front door, working the bell pull. I hurried my pace, anxious to see him again, and confide in him what I had heard.

Alice opened the front door. A moment later she shook her head, but then, seeing me coming up the drive, pointed in my direction. Will turned, and despite my reduced condition, I felt myself blushing a little at the way he reacted when he saw me. He came down the steps and strode out to meet me.

'Rosemary!' he said. 'I thought I'd come back to see how you are.'

'As you can see, I went for a walk,' I replied. 'There's quite a charming little peninsula just beyond those trees.'

He nodded and fell into step beside me as we continued to walk toward the house. 'I've visited it,' he said. 'It's called Shimmering Top.'

'I should have guessed you would know that,' I smiled. 'How were the children when they got to school?'

'They couldn't get into that class-room quickly enough!' he answered. 'And on the way there they couldn't speak highly enough of old Miss Twickenham.'

'I liked her from the start.'

'Well,' he said, 'how are you feeling now?'

'Fine.'

'You don't *look* it.'

'Thank you, kind sir.'

'I didn't mean it like that. But what with fainting yesterday . . . '

'I told you, I'm fine. Just . . . tired, that's all.'

'Just that?' he asked, searching my profile closely.

'Well . . . '

'Tell me how you feel,' he prompted.

I considered for a moment, then said, 'Well, like the children, I have had an upset stomach. And I feel a little stiff and breathless.'

'You've never felt like that before?'

I began to feel uneasy, then. 'I appreciate your concern, Will, but . . . '

And then the world began to swim away from me again, and even as I felt my eyelids fluttering, he reached out and caught me, and once more I fell limp into his arms.

He carried me easily the rest of the way. I remember hearing the crunch of gravel beneath his feet, and then Alice's voice, demanding, 'What happened?'

'She's fainted,' said Will. And then he was striding across the checkerboard floor of the foyer, footsteps echoing briskly. 'Where's her room?' he demanded.

'You can't go upstairs!' protested Alice.

'Take me there,' he snapped, his voice low and authoritative. '*Now.*'

I opened my eyes and whispered, 'I'm . . . all right . . . '

'You are no such thing,' he said, looking down at me with such intensity that, even in my weakened state, I was taken aback.

A moment later I was back in the Green Suite and he was settling me gently onto the bed. I began to feel my faculties returning and tried to sit up, but he stopped me with a gesture and then, seeing the carafe of water on the dresser, went to pour me a glass. He stopped almost at once and heeled around to face Alice. 'This water is filthy,' he said. 'Fetch some fresh water, if you please.'

From the door, Alice's mouth dropped open. 'I can't leave you alone with — '

'I do not intend to ask you again,' he said firmly.

Backing down, Alice gave me a look, then took the tray upon which the carafe and glasses were set, and left the room. After she had gone, Will examined the suite, and I watched as he wiped a finger across the dust that Jane must have left behind her. At last he came to me and sat at my side.

'You'll be all right now,' he said, but his expression was grim.

'I *feel* all right now,' I replied.

'Yes . . . until the next time.'

Looking up at him, I suddenly felt very frightened. 'What's wrong with me?' I asked. 'Do you know?'

'I believe I do,' he replied. 'But you're going to be all right now, Rosemary. That's all that matters.'

He took my hand in his and it seemed like the most natural thing in the world.

'Who *are* you?' I asked.

Perhaps it was my imagination, but he seemed to tense. 'What do you mean?'

'Well . . . I know you're a writer. But are you also a doctor?'

He relaxed again. 'Oh, no — I'm not that clever! I told you — I'm just a collector of useless and sometimes not-so-useless information.'

'I think you're more than that. And you *are* clever.'

He smiled a little sadly. 'If I was as clever as all that,' he said, 'I would have lived life a little differently.'

'What does that mean?'

Before he could answer, Hayden

Cross stormed into the room, followed by Kaylock and, behind him, Alice. Cross looked from Will to me, and then said, 'What is the meaning of this!'

Will stood up. 'Mrs. Shaw fainted. I fetched her up here so that she might recover.'

'Well, she appears to have done exactly that,' Cross replied tightly. 'You may go now, Mr. Hennessey.'

Ignoring him, Will looked at Alice. 'Did you fetch fresh water?'

'Yes, sir,' Alice answered hesitantly.

Will indicated that she should set the tray down on the dresser, then went to it, inspected the water and poured me a glass.

'I asked you to go, Mr. Hennessey,' Cross reminded him. 'Will you do so, or should I have you forcibly ejected?'

Kaylock grunted. He appeared to relish such a prospect.

Will stood his ground. 'I will leave in due course,' he replied. 'But before I do so, I have a request to make of you, Mr. Cross — that you will find Mrs. Shaw alternative accommodation for the remainder of her stay here.'

'*What?*'

'Her present surroundings do not agree with either her or her children,' Will replied, his tone brooking no argument. 'I will therefore thank you to find her some other rooms. I am sure you have plenty to choose from in a house of this size.'

'Who are you to make such demands?' roared Cross. 'You have already sullied this woman's reputation by being with her in her rooms without a chaperone! Get out of here at once!'

Beside him, Kaylock took a threatening step forward, but still Will stood his ground. I struggled up and said, 'Please, Will. Don't make any trouble — '

'There won't be any trouble,' said Will, still looking at Cross. 'Mr. Cross will be happy to change your accommodations. If not, we can always call in a doctor from Phoenix Port. I'm sure he will recommend the same thing — a new suite . . . and *one that isn't green.*'

Those last words were spoken through gritted teeth, and for reasons I did not then understand, Cross almost blanched.

'Will you grant me this one request, Mr. Cross?' prompted Will.

Grudgingly, Cross nodded. Clearing his throat, he said, 'Of . . . of course. Mrs. Shaw's wellbeing is my primary concern.'

'Then I thank you,' said Will. 'And I bid you good-day.'

8

That afternoon, our few possessions were transferred to another suite of rooms farther along the hallway. Though these quarters were of a more sober design, they were comfortable enough, and I was happy with the exchange. Indeed, as the afternoon wore on, I began to feel more like my old self again, and at four o'clock that afternoon was waiting on the steps when the Phaeton came along the drive, bringing my children home to me.

I was delighted to see that their second day at school had done nothing to diminish their enthusiasm. As Will lifted them down, they threw themselves at me, both vying to tell me what they had done that day, and to show me the paintings they had created that morning.

'How are you feeling, Rosemary?' Will asked when the children finally fell quiet.

'Much better,' I said sincerely. 'Though I have no idea why a room should make me feel ill, any more than a change of rooms should make me feel better.'

'But you *do* feel better?'

'Yes.'

'And Cross *did* change your accommodations, as I asked?'

'Yes — though to me it sounded more like a demand that a request.'

He smiled a little self-consciously. 'Well, for that I apologize. I try always to be scrupulously polite . . . but . . . well, though I have no right to say so, I feel very protective of you.'

'It's odd,' I replied, flattered that he should feel that way, 'but ever since we've been here, I've felt the *need* to be protected, and I don't know why.'

Jonathan tugged at my skirts. 'Can we see Shimmering Top?' he asked.

I looked at Will.

'My fault, I'm afraid,' he confessed. 'I told them you'd discovered a special secret place this morning, called Shimmering Top.'

'Can we?' asked Frances.

I nodded. 'Just let me go inside and get a coat.'

As I turned back to the house, I saw Hayden Cross watching us from one of the ground-floor windows. His expression, as his eyes bored into mine, was impossible to decipher, but nevertheless, sent a shiver through me.

I hurried to our new suite, got my coat and went back downstairs. Cross was waiting for me in the foyer.

'Going out, Mrs. Shaw?' he enquired.

'I'm taking the children to Shimmering Top,' I replied. 'I shan't be long.'

'May I assume that Mr. Hennessey is going with you as well?' he prompted.

'Yes.'

'Do you not see any harm in that?'

'No harm at all,' I said honestly.

'And no disrespect? To your late husband's memory, I mean?'

That angered me, and I was glad, for the anger dispelled some of the fear with which I now seemed to live almost constantly. 'I thought we had discussed this yesterday,' I said. 'Mr. Hennessey is a friend and nothing more.'

'You don't honestly *believe* that?'

'I have no reason to doubt it.'

'Then you have obviously been blind to the way he looks at you,' Cross replied. 'And for your part, are you seriously telling me you have no feelings for this man?'

'Of course I have feelings. He is a wonderful man. And he has shown a genuine interest in my welfare.'

'Don't you find that at all ... strange, Mrs. Shaw?'

'Not at all. Why should I?'

'I have been in business for a great many years,' he said. 'And it has always been my experience that very little is ever given freely. It is in man's nature to give, only that he might also receive.'

I shook my head. 'You're talking in riddles, Mr. Cross.'

'Then let me make myself clear. You came here in the expectation that you would receive a home and money — money that was intended to pay off your late husband's debts. Suppose someone else got wind of that, and came here ahead of you, with the intention of . . . romancing . . . you until you *received* that money. Once he was in your affections, he would have little problem relieving you of it.'

'Mr. Hennessey is not that kind of man.'

'How can you be so sure?'

'As I said before, I am a good judge of character. In any case, I will *not* be receiving any money now, will I?'

'But does *he* know that?'

'I'm sorry you have such a cynical approach to life, Mr. Cross. But it has always been *my* experience that not everyone is quite as mercenary as you seem to suppose.'

'Ah, but you would say that, wouldn't you?'

'What does *that* mean?'

'I have seen the way you look at him, too,' he said. 'You're in love with him, aren't you? Hopelessly infatuated with a man you hardly know.'

His tone was thick with disgust.

I didn't want to blush, but I felt my cheeks color anyway. 'I do not give my heart *quite* that freely, Mr. Cross,' I said stiffly. But in Will, I realized that I *had* given him my heart. Even though there was no future in our relationship, I had surrendered body and soul to him because he represented everything that was good and right in a man.

'Well, have a care,' said Cross. 'In my opinion, he is not all he makes himself out to be. And that makes him dangerous, madam. Very dangerous indeed.'

He turned on his heel and strode back to the sitting room. I watched him close the door behind him and wondered again about the conversation I had overheard the night before.

Who is he, and where did he come from? Cross had asked.

Does it matter? This from Kaylock.

I wish I knew. But one thing is certain — we didn't allow for this.

So what do you want me to do?

Find out everything you can about this man Hennessey. But be careful about it. We don't want to tip our hand.

Had Cross been confiding his suspicions about Will to Kaylock? Was that why he had ordered Kaylock to find out everything he could about Will — to make sure he *wasn't* a conman, out to rob me of money he thought I was coming into? I simply did not believe that Will was the kind of man Cross believed him to be. In any case, that still didn't explain Cross's reference to *we didn't allow for this*, or *we don't want to tip our hand.*

I went back outside. Will and the children were waiting for me in the coming sunset. Together we crossed the lane, passed through the trees and followed the winding path between wild blackberry bushes and scarlet burning bush. The children raced on ahead, with instructions not to go too far, and to stop well before they got anywhere near the edge of the cliff.

The late afternoon was cool and the air smelled of myrtle and bellflowers. Hummingbirds were still busy collecting pollen, and from up ahead there came the constant, busy *shush* of the sea. I glanced at Will's profile, not wanting to think ill of him, but knowing I must satisfy my growing curiosity about this man who had so unexpectedly come into my life.

'What did you mean earlier?' I asked. 'When you said you wished you had lived your life differently?'

He shook his head. 'Nothing.'

'Please, Will. I want to know.'

'I was just feeling sorry for myself,' he said dismissively.

'I can't imagine you ever doing *that*.'

'Oh, I do, believe me.'

'Why?'

He hesitated, then said, 'When I was ten years old, there was an outbreak of yellow fever where we lived in Philadelphia. It wasn't anywhere near as bad as the epidemic that wiped out thousands of people there in 1793, but bad enough. Both my parents and my little sister died.

'Our family had never been what you might call well-off, and I knew that my aunts and uncles could ill afford another mouth to feed. So I left home — not that I really had a home to leave, by then. I went on the drift and to my surprise, I found that I actually enjoyed it.

'Of course, it wasn't all good — I froze in winter, was soaked to the skin every time there was a downpour and no shelter to be had. Sometimes I went hungry for days on end, and had to look after myself whenever I fell ill . . . but every so often I'd find a job and earn enough money to eat well and buy such supplies as I needed. Sleeping out on summer nights beneath a roof full of stars, knowing only that tomorrow would bring me fresh sights and experiences, never another worry about going to school, educating myself as I went along . . .

'You might find it hard to believe, Rosemary, but even though I was little more than an urchin, I felt like a king. I thought I would wander forever, and for years I did just that, never staying in any one place too long, never setting down roots and never wanting to. I was a nomad, and proud of it.

'But sooner or later you realize there's a price to pay for the life I led — a heavy one. It's called loneliness. By the time I was sixteen I had gathered more experience than many a full-grown man. I could survive in almost any environment and knew well how to live off the land. But where's the sense of living a life if you can't *share* it? I had no friends, no family I could return to, not even a casual acquaintance with whom to pass the time of day. And the older I grew, the heavier that burden seemed to weigh on me.

'Somewhere along the way I realized

I had tired of my wandering life, and come to envy the people who had homes, and jobs, and loved ones. They had order in their lives — I had none. I belonged to no place in particular, and had precious little to offer any companion who might come my way, save a knowledge of odd facts. I *did* find a job, eventually, which enabled me to earn a decent wage and live a little more like the folk around me. But even here I was constantly on the move, travelling wherever my work took me, and though I enjoyed the work, I could ask no one else to put up with the long absences it entailed, even if I could *find* someone. In the end, I tried to convince myself that I was probably better off as a loner. And I've been a loner ever since.'

We stopped walking and I turned to look at him. 'Oh, Will. That is so sad.'

'It is what it is,' he replied. 'And don't misunderstand me. I'm not complaining. I chose to drift and I enjoyed it. But had I been as clever as you seem to think I am, I would have realized much sooner that it was no way to live, not really. Unfortunately, I wised up just a little too late.'

'It's never too late,' I replied.

He looked down at me, and his voice seemed to a drop a little.

'Perhaps it isn't, at that,' he said.

I found myself gazing up into his green eyes. In them I saw nothing of greed, or deceit. What I saw was a kind of pain, as if he really *did* regret the footloose life he'd led, that he really *did* envy those whose lives were settled and orderly. He looked tired of constantly being on the move . . . he looked like a man who had never loved but wanted that more than anything, that he had so much to give and had never yet been afforded the opportunity to give it: and seeing all that, I knew without a single shadow of doubt that Hayden Cross had been right . . . I *did* love Will.

He must have seen as much in the way I looked at him, for his hands came up and his fingers curled gently around my upper arms, and even as my face tilted upward, his came slowly down toward me. I felt the heat coming off his skin, despite the chill of the late afternoon, smelled the bay rum on his strong, square jaw . . .

And then, suddenly, he turned from me, and, following his gaze, I was just in time to see the rustle and sway of a nearby burning bush. The lines of his face grew sober.

'I might have guessed it,' he muttered. 'Cross must have sent that ape of his to spy on us.'

Above the pounding of the sea, I heard the sound of someone pushing through undergrowth, away from us.

'Kaylock,' I said. And then, 'Mr. Cross thinks you're only after me for my money.'

He returned his attention to me. 'Does he, indeed?'

'He has instructed Kaylock to find out everything he can about you.'

He grinned. 'I know.'

'*What?*'

'Earlier today, Mason, who runs the

hotel, told me a man as wide as a wagon and slightly smaller than a mountain had come in to ask after me. There wasn't much Mason could tell him, and the man — obviously Kaylock — went on his way. But when I checked my room later, I knew that someone had been in there ahead of me, and searched through my belongings. My guess is that he must have used the firestairs at the back of the hotel to gain entrance to my room through the window.'

'But . . . but doesn't that concern you?' I asked.

'Of course it concerns me. But I'm pretty sure he left knowing as much — or as little — about me as he did when he arrived.' He sobered again. 'What do *you* think, anyway? Do *you* think I'm after your money?'

'What money?' I replied.

His grin came back. 'The truth, Rosemary?' he asked. 'I wouldn't care if you were the poorest pauper on the face of God's earth. But . . . I know I have no right to feel about you the way I do.'

'Nor I you,' I confessed in a whisper. 'But perhaps when this is all over, and a suitable period of mourning has passed . . . ?'

His smile was strangely bittersweet. 'Let's cross that bridge when we come to it,' he advised. 'You don't know what's in your future, yet. It might be something so grand that there will be no room in it for me.'

'There will *always* be room for you,' I assured him.

We looked at each other for a moment longer, and then, with effort, he shrugged off his sudden melancholy. 'Now — where are those children?' he called.

'Here we are!' cried Jonathan, as he and Frances came racing back toward us.

Will went forward to meet them. 'Did you know the Atlantic is the second largest ocean in the world?' he asked them. 'No? Well, then allow me to tell you all about the creatures who call it home! There are manatees and sea lions, humpback whales and even ghost crabs!'

I watched the three of them walking toward Shimmering Top, three silhouettes against an amber sunset, and though two of them were mine, I wished with all my heart that all three were.

★ ★ ★

We left Will at the front steps. Dusk was falling fast by this time, powdering the sky with a deep, star-picked purple, the lowering sun daubing the underbellies of the clouds a delicate pink.

'Look after your mother, you two,' he told the children, and when he looked at me he lowered his voice and added, 'Be careful, Rosemary. I fear there's a storm coming tonight. But like all storms, it will leave the air cleaner and fresher for its passing.'

I frowned up at him. 'Another riddle,' I said.

'I'm sorry?'

'Oh, nothing. It seems to have been my day for riddles, that's all,' I said. But I puzzled over what he had said, and what he'd meant by it, as he climbed onto the Phaeton and turned it back toward Phoenix Port, and I felt the poorer when he finally vanished from our sight.

We went inside and I took the children upstairs to prepare for the evening meal. We dined alone that evening — where Cross had gone to, I had no idea. Afterwards, we retired to our new suite — which met with the children's immediate approval — and I took out a book of fairy stories I had packed before leaving Connecticut, and began to read to them.

An hour passed in this fashion, until there came a soft knocking at the door. When I answered it, I found Jane waiting just beyond the threshold.

'Sorry to disturb you, ma'am,' she said.

'That's all right,' I replied, and just to

tease her, added, 'Don't tell me you've come to clean the room.'

She frowned, then shook her head. 'Uh, no, ma'am. Alice asked me to deliver this. She said she received it from your . . . ah . . . gentleman caller, a few moments ago.'

She handed me a sealed envelope upon which my name had been written in neat copperplate script.

'Thank you,' I said, accepting it with more than a little surprise.

I closed the door and tore open the envelope. It contained a single sheet of paper upon which had been written a short message:

Rosemary —
   Meet me as soon as you can at Shimmering Top. It's important. I'll be waiting.

It was signed, *Will*.

I read it through once more, trying to understand what it might mean. Unable to do so, I quickly opened the door again and was just in time to catch Jane before she reached the head of the stairs.

'Jane!' I called.

She hurried back.

'Yes, ma'am?'

'I have to go out briefly,' I explained. 'Will you look after the children until I get back?'

She smiled. 'Of course, ma'am. I'd be happy to.'

'So would we,' called Frances. 'We *like* Jane.'

I quickly took my coat from the wardrobe and hurriedly shrugged into it, stuffing the note into one of the pockets as I did so. Still thinking about the note and what was so important that Will had asked me to meet him at Shimmering Top, I said distractedly, 'You should feel privileged, Jane. There isn't much about Rosehaven that the children have found to like so far.'

Again the chubby young girl showed confusion. 'Rosehaven, ma'am?' she asked.

I nodded. 'This place,' I said.

Her frown only deepened. 'I think there must be some mistake, ma'am,' she said. 'This house doesn't have a name, and certainly not one as pretty as Rosehaven. In fact, I never even *heard* that name until you just mentioned it.'

9

As I stepped out into the early evening, a fork of lightning many miles out to sea sliced down through the ebon sky, even as a chilly wind picked up and tore at the tails of my coat. I reached up to hold my lapels together at my neck and set off along the drive toward Shimmering Top, the only light coming from the full moon above. Now that I really thought about it, I had no memory of leaving our suite, descending the stairs and letting myself out. My thoughts had been firmly focused upon Jane's revelation that this house was not called Rosehaven at all, and never had been. But what did that really signify? What was really going on in this wretched place?

I had gone perhaps twenty yards, no more, when I had the uneasy but unshakable feeling that I was being watched. I stopped and turned, and was just in time to see a drape fall back across the sitting room window and obscure the bar of lamplight that had shown there . . . that, and the unmistakable silhouette of Hayden Cross.

I hurried on, wanting to see Will and hear what he had to say that was so important, and then I wanted to get back to my children, to be with them on this of all nights and seriously consider leaving on the morrow and never coming back. Of course, the prospect of never seeing Will again broke my heart — the children would miss him, too, for they had come to think the world of him — but it was as he had said, we had no right to feel about each other as we did. It was ridiculous, for one cannot help falling in love, and certainly cannot control the timing of it, but convention was convention, and I had no desire to show John any of the disrespect that Cross had insinuated earlier.

I crossed the lane and began to hurry

through the trees that now swayed back and forth in the strengthening wind. Night creatures scuttled through the dark shadows, and I started at every sudden sound they made. Up ahead another fork of lightning cleaved the sky, though there was neither thunder nor rain . . . yet.

I pushed on, struggling a little now in the stormy conditions, until I heard a sudden sound behind me. I spun around, and though I could not be sure, I thought I saw a shadow some forty yards behind me suddenly dodge sideways, off the path and into the cover of the timber.

Now I was thoroughly terrified, for that shadow had been massive, and I felt that it could only belong to Kaylock.

More anxious than ever to see Will, I continued on, breaking into a little trot now. And behind me, I heard the odd shift of bushes being thrust out of the path of whoever was following me, and the occasional crack my pursuer made accidentally snapping a twig underfoot.

Before me, the path continued to unwind. In my haste, I stumbled over the uneven ground but somehow kept going, knowing that Will would be waiting for me at Shimmering Top itself, and that once I was with him, I would be safe.

Breathless, I followed another turn in the path and there it was, the place where Will had asked me to meet him.

But as lightning briefly illuminated the cliff before me, I saw that Will was not there!

The area was deserted.

I opened my mouth to call Will's name, but before I could, I heard the heavy steps of my pursuer — Kaylock — coming ever closer. I had a sudden, sickening feeling that the note from Will been nothing more than a fabrication, a ruse to lure me out here where Kaylock could . . . could *what*? *What* did this man have in mind for me?

I only knew one thing for certain — I could go no further, for all that lay before me now was the cliff edge. And to go back meant I would have to meet Kaylock coming from the opposite direction.

And then, without warning, someone grabbed my arm.

Instinctively I went to cry out, but my assailant's other hand closed around my mouth, silencing me. I was dragged backwards, into the bushes, and there was not one single thing I could do to stop it.

Then I heard a voice whisper in my ear.

'Be quiet, Rosemary! It's all right!'

I felt faint. It was Will.

I turned to him and opened my mouth to speak, but he silenced me with a gesture, and indicated that I should keep watching the path from the relative safety of our hiding place. A few seconds later the moonlight showed us Kaylock, striding slowly into view. He was dressed for the weather, in the greatcoat that made him appear even larger than he was, and the muffler that hid his hideous lantern jaw and long beak of nose. He stamped right past us and cautiously went closer to the cliff edge. There he stopped and looked first left, then right. Clearly he was wondering what had become of me.

He made a sound of frustration low in his throat and turned around. And that was when I saw what he was holding in his right hand — a knife!

As moonlight flickered off the long blade, I almost gasped, but again, Will put his hand across my mouth to silence any cry. Still, there could no longer be any doubt. That man meant me harm!

'Stay here,' Will whispered, and before I could react, he sprang from the bushes to confront the giant.

'It's over,' he said. 'Give it up, Kaylock.'

The giant, recognizing him, only gave another grunt. 'Who *are* you?' he asked, his voice little more than a rumble.

He didn't really want to know — the

question was only meant as a distraction. For in the very next moment he threw himself at Will, the knife flashing in a deadly silver arc before him. I cried out, but Will had already leapt back, out of reach of the blade, and now the two men were circling warily, and Will was unbuttoning his jacket, never once taking his eyes from his opponent.

Once again Kaylock hurled himself at Will. Will sidestepped as nimbly as any matador, and Kaylock went stumbling past. While Kaylock was still off-balance, Will tore his jacket off and swiftly wrapped it around his right hand. As Kaylock made a dreadful stabbing motion with the knife, Will whirled the jacket by one sleeve, and even as I watched, it seemed to wrap itself around Kaylock's arm. Will yanked, and Kaylock stumbled forward. Will struck him on the jaw, and the giant was so stunned by the blow that he released his hold on the knife, which fell to the grass.

But he was far from finished. Now he

swung his huge fists, first left, then right, but Will ducked and dodged every blow. Angry now, Kaylock came at him in a rush, but Will had expected that. He blocked Kaylock's punch and struck again with his other fist.

Almost before I knew what I was doing, I broke free of our little hiding place and yelled at them to stop, but all I did was succeed in breaking Will's concentration. Darting me a look, he yelled, 'Go back to the house! Go back and lock yourself in your room!'

Kaylock caught him then, lifted him in a savage bear hug. Will's face screwed up at the pain of it, but then he clapped his hands against Kaylock's ears, and Kaylock dropped him and roared at the agony of the blow.

Still they fought, and with every move and counter-move, they seemed to come closer to the edge of the cliff. I felt powerless, and hated the feeling. But what could I do?

And then Kaylock launched a right hook that would have finished the contest there and then, had it landed. But once again Will ducked beneath the blow, and Kaylock's momentum carried him around and backwards.

His heels touched the jagged earth that formed the edge of the cliff. His dark eyes went wide, and at last I saw an emotion within them — fear. His arms windmilled, but he was already too late to regain his balance. Will reached for him, called, '*Take my hand!*' But Kaylock had no chance to grab this precious lifeline . . . he was already falling.

He did not cry out, but went silently to his doom . . . and it was this silence that was more chilling than anything else.

Lightning scored the sky, and at last, far out to sea, I heard the first rumble of thunder.

Will turned to me and he looked spent, not so much from the fight, but that he hadn't been able to save Kaylock from his grisly death. I picked up his fallen jacket and took it to him, and he looked at me and then I went into his arms and let him hold me. I felt him press me close to him, and knew he was relieved that I was safe, and there for him.

After another moment, we broke apart and he put his jacket back on. 'Come on,' he said softly, and putting his arm around me, led us back along the winding path between the wind-whipped bushes.

'What . . . why did you ask me to meet you here?' I asked.

He looked at me. 'I didn't.'

'But I have a note . . . '

'I didn't write it. That was most likely Cross.'

'And yet . . . you were here. Waiting for me.'

He shook his head. 'I *followed* you from the house and when it became clear where you were going, I got here ahead of you.'

I stopped suddenly, and unable to hold my emotions in check any longer, suddenly sobbed. 'Oh, Will! What is *happening* here?'

He held me again. 'I'll explain everything in due course,' he said. 'But for now, take heart in the fact that whatever it was, it's *over*.'

We started walking again. 'Why did that . . . that man try to kill me?'

'Remember the day Kaylock tormented you and the children with those shears of his?' Will asked.

I studied him more closely. 'What do you know about that?'

'Do you recall that he stopped and stared off into the woods when he heard the snap of a branch?'

'Yes. It . . . it gave us the chance to get away from him.'

'I was the one who snapped the branch, to distract him,' Will explained. 'I don't know that he would have done anything to you . . . then. I believe that Hayden Cross was hoping that Kaylock's threatening behavior might scare you all the way back to Connecticut . . . if the Green Suite didn't save him the bother first.'

Now I felt absolutely lost. 'I don't understand any of this,' I said. 'What do you mean, about the Green Suite?'

'Cross tried to poison you,' he said softly. 'And very nearly succeeded.'

'*What?*'

'It's a little-known fact that arsenic is used in the production of wallpapers as vividly green as the one that was used in the Green Suite,' he explained grimly. 'Because the symptoms of arsenic poisoning can mimic those of diphtheria, the connection isn't always made. Of course, Cross tried to speed the process up by sending a maid in every day to dust the walls. In effect, she was unwittingly dislodging the poison from the paper so that it would be in the air you breathed and the water you drank.'

I could hardly believe anyone could be so callous.

'Well, thanks to my penchant for collecting so much seemingly useless data, I was able to see the thing as it really was.'

'Then insisting upon having me moved to different quarters really did save my life . . . and the lives of Jonathan and Frances!'

'Yes. And it also forced Cross's hand. Since he couldn't rely on the arsenic to finish you, he ordered Kaylock to arrange an accident for you here, on Shimmering Top. It wouldn't be the first such 'accident' Kaylock has arranged. He has — had — a criminal record that goes back well over a decade, most of it involving violence.'

I shuddered.

'And . . . and my children?' I whispered. 'What was to h-happen to them?'

Will didn't answer, except to point ahead and say, 'We're here. And I have the Phaeton hidden at the side of the house. We'll soon have you all away from here, now.'

'I never want to see this place again,' I said. 'But I *do* want answers, Will.'

He squeezed me. 'And you'll get them,' he promised grimly.

The Brougham was parked outside

the house. Seeing it, Will laughed bitterly. 'It looks as if Cross is planning to be somewhere else when you 'disappear'. He's probably had his alibi in place for some time now.'

We climbed the steps and went inside. Alice, hearing the door close behind us, appeared in the kitchen doorway. Seeing us, she turned to go back to the servants' quarters, but Will stopped her.

'You can pack your things and leave,' he said. 'There'll be no job for you here after tonight.'

She frowned. 'What?'

'You heard me,' he said. 'Now, pack your things and go, and be grateful I don't have you arrested for conspiracy to commit murder.'

Her skin turned as pale as milk. 'I . . . I don't . . . ' she stammered.

Ignoring her, Will led us to the sitting room. With barely a pause, he threw the doors open and together we marched inside even as thunder crashed overhead, and the rain finally began to fall.

Hayden Cross had been standing before the fireplace, drumming his fingers on the mantelpiece, when we entered. Startled, he now spun around and stared at us.

'What is the — ' he began.

'You're finished, Mr. Cross,' said Will. '*It*'s finished.'

'What are you talking about?' he blustered. 'Get out of here!'

'You lied to Mrs. Shaw, you tried to poison her and her children with arsenic, and when that proved to be too slow a process, you decided to have Kaylock push Mrs. Shaw over the cliff to her doom in a tragic 'accident',' Will continued implacably. 'What about the children, Mr. Cross? Jonathan and Frances? Are you so heartless that you were going to kill them, too? Or have them placed in care a thousand miles from here?'

Cross was silent.

Beside me, Will shook his head in disgust.

'And what makes it even worse,' he

said, 'is that — '

'You can't prove it,' Cross interrupted. 'You can't prove a thing in a court of law.'

'I don't have to,' Will replied. 'My word is good enough for Joseph Trent.'

Startled by the comment, Cross's ice-chip eyes narrowed fractionally. 'Are you saying you know Joseph?'

'I work for him,' Will responded. 'You see, you weren't as clever as you thought you were, Mr. Cross, Joseph Trent trusted you for years. And for years he stood by you as only a genuine friend could. He forgave you for every low-handed thing you ever did or tried to do, and always in the hope that you would learn your lesson and become a better person for it.

'But the day he informed you of his intention to invite Mrs. Shaw to Rosehaven, he saw something in your reaction that he didn't like. And so he acted upon it, and was right to do so.'

'I'm sure I have no idea what you are talking about.'

'Then we'll go,' said Will, taking me by the arm. 'In the meantime, I am instructed to tell you that Mr. Trent will be taking steps to dissolve your partnership immediately. If you know what's good for you, you'll leave this place and never return. If you do, Mr. Trent will prosecute you to the full extent of the law.'

We turned and started back toward the door. I was still in shock, emotionally numb and struggling to take everything in . . . or as little of it as I had learned so far. It seemed to me that while I was here, in this house, in the presence of the man, this *stranger* who had tried so hard to kill me, I would never be able to gather my thoughts and understand what had happened, or why. Just then I wanted only to gather my children and leave this place and then make sense of everything — if I could.

But without warning Cross snapped, 'You're not going anywhere!'

We stopped, turned back . . . and

when Will saw the gun in Hayden Cross's hand, he at once stepped in front of me. 'Don't be a fool,' he said. 'Consider yourself lucky to have gotten off so lightly. If it were up to me . . . '

'But it isn't, is it?' sneered Cross. 'Joseph need never learn the truth. I could offer to bribe you to keep your silence, but I doubt you are the kind of man I could buy. Even if I could, I would leave myself open to blackmail at any time in the future, and I have no intentions of doing that.'

'So you're going to kill us,' said Will.

'I've seen the way you two have looked at each other ever since you've been here, just how protective of Mrs. Shaw you are, Hennessey. You *are* in love with her, aren't you?'

Silence followed the question. But it lasted for only a moment until Will said, 'Yes.'

'Then who's to say you didn't two fall in love and simply decide to leave this place together, never to be seen again?'

166

'Joseph Trent will never believe that.'

'Whether he believes it or not is of no concern to me. He can never disprove it.'

Will shook his head. 'I've met many evil men in my time,' he said. 'But you are by far the most evil man of them all.'

I sensed a tightening of his shoulders and knew he was going to do something that might only hasten our fate. I heard myself whisper, 'Will . . . '

But I was too late. He was already moving.

10

Even as he leapt forward, he pushed me sideways, so that I stumbled and dropped to the carpet and out of the gun's line of fire. I screamed as Hayden Cross brought the gun up and flame spat from its barrel. The sound of the shot was tremendous within the confines of the room. But then Will collided with him and they were locked in a struggle, and I realized with relief that in his haste, Cross had missed Will.

I climbed to my feet as the gun fell from Cross's fingers and thumped to the rug. My only thought was to snatch it up and yell at them to stop fighting. It wasn't for Cross that I was worried, it was for Will, my dear, caring, loving Will, and it terrified me to the core that I might lose him even as I had just found him.

Then Cross lashed out with a wild

punch. It caught Will a glancing blow and flung him to one side. Before he could recover, Cross looked around, spotted the gun and reached out to snatch it up.

I did the only thing I could — I brought the heel of my shoe down on his outspread hand, and he howled in a mixture of pain and rage and quickly withdrew his hand, which I saw my heel had cut open. He glared at me and in that split second, when no more than two feet separated us, I saw sheer hatred in his eyes for me. But *why?* Why did he hate me so?

And then Will began to push up from the kneeling position into which he had fallen, and hearing as much, Cross turned, snatched up one of the chopped logs stacked beside the fire and raised it above his head, intending to strike him with it.

'*Will!*'

Without thinking, I threw myself at Cross, tore the log from his hands, and as he turned again to face me, I swung it with all my might. The log caught him only a glancing blow, but he saw in me the primitive urge to protect the thing I loved, and it scared him. With a curse, he ran from the room before I could attempt to hit him again.

'Rosemary!'

It was Will's voice, and the sound of it brought something like sanity back to me.

He said, 'Go and join the children, and take that gun with you — '

'What about you?'

'I'm going after him!' he declared.

He left the room at a run, and caught up in the moment, I followed him. Our hurried footsteps clattered across the checkerboard floor, and then all we could hear was another terrific clash of thunder that made the windows buzz and vibrate in their frames.

The front door hung open — lightning threw a sudden, white glare across the foyer. Will glanced over his shoulder and said, 'Stay with the children, I said!'

But I knew Jonathan and Frances would be safe with Jane, and my place now, I felt, was with Will — my *man*.

With hardly a care for his own safety, Will burst out into the full force of the storm. At once rain lashed his face and plastered his raven-black hair down over his forehead. As I joined him, I was just in time to see Cross climb up onto the high seat of the Brougham, and flick the whip over the horses' backs as if he were demented.

And it came to me then that he probably was. Whatever plan he had set in motion had been destroyed. Now all that remained for him was escape.

The Brougham turned crazily onto the road to Phoenix Port, and for one heart-stopping moment I thought it would overturn. At what seemed like the last moment, it righted itself and vanished from sight.

Will turned to face me, his skin beaded with rain. 'Woman!' he said in frustration. 'Go inside!'

Before I could reply, he hurried down

the steps and around the house to the Phaeton, and once again I went after him. Lifting my skirts high, I climbed the wheel and joined him on the seat. He looked at me, opened his mouth to issue a rebuke, then saw the futility of it and offered me a tight smile instead.

Then he was using the reins, and with a cry of, '*Yaaahhh!*' the carriage lurched off in pursuit.

I clung to the rail for dear life as we took the turn onto the village road and the carriage tilted drunkenly, then slammed back down onto all four wheels. Through the driving rain I could just make out the Brougham, as it raced on ahead. Another searing flash of lightning showed us that the two-horse team were steadily drawing ahead of us — that we stood no real chance of catching up with Cross.

The carriage gave another lurch as it the wheels lost traction on the road's rain-slick surface, and now I clung to Will — Will, who had been my tower of strength through this entire, ghastly ordeal. Thunder boomed overhead and the horse flicked its head in fear.

'Give it up, Will!' I called above the storm. 'We'll never catch him now!'

He gave me a quick glance — it had to be quick, for he needed all his attention on the treacherous road before us. But in that moment I saw in him the knowledge that I was right — we would never even come close to Cross now . . . and yet there was also a stubborn resistance in him to concede defeat.

Another flare of lightning ripped across the sky, and up ahead we saw the Brougham begin to somehow . . . teeter. The wheels were spinning, but finding no grip, and to make the matter worse, the two-horse team had yielded to full panic. As they ran even harder, the Brougham itself began to lose its center of gravity. Even as thunder followed the lightning, we saw that every sway of the vehicle seemed to make it tilt to one side, then the other, that little bit more.

And then —

Even as we watched, the Brougham crashed over onto its side. The wagon shaft snapped with a dreadful wrench and splintering of wood, and the horses, now free of the Brougham's weight, galloped off into the night.

Carried along by momentum, the Brougham itself slid along on its side for several yards before finally coming to a halt. As we approached it, a brief flash of lightning showed Hayden Cross, soaked to the skin, climbing unsteadily to his feet. He saw us approaching, threw a quick, desperate glance around him, and then ran toward a low hedge that separated the road from the tobacco field beyond it.

Beside me, Will rammed his foot on the brake handle and the carriage slewed to a halt. Standing up, he put his hands to his mouth and yelled, 'Cross! Don't be a fool!'

But once again, Cross paid him no mind. He leapt over the hedge with an agility that belied his age, and began to slip and splash desperately across the field, flattening knee-high tobacco plants as he went.

Thunder rumbled overhead and the rain began to fall even harder. Again Will cried, 'Cross! Cross, get out of that field!'

Now I doubted he could hear us at all.

I reached up, took Will's arm, and when he turned his rain-pebbled face down to me, I said tiredly, 'Leave it, Will. Let him get away.'

He looked at me strangely. 'He won't get away,' he muttered.

I frowned. 'What do you — '

But before I could finish the question, the brightest, fiercest fork of lightning split the sky, a crash of thunder following almost instantly, and Will quickly pulled me close to him, wrapped his arms around me and I buried my head against his chest . . . though not before I saw what happened next.

The lightning did not strike the earth

— it struck Hayden Cross. It happened in one blinding split second, and there could be no avoiding it. Cross dropped as if pole-axed, and lay still in the mud, a few lazy spirals of smoke rising up from his body.

'My God,' I sobbed. 'My God . . .'

Tiredly, Will said, 'That's what I was trying to tell him. A tobacco field is the last place you want to be in a storm like this. I don't know why it is, but the tobacco somehow acts as a conductor. It *attracts* the lightning to it.'

'Will . . .' I managed.

'Shhhh,' he said, holding me closer, protecting me as best he could against the wild night. 'It's over now, Rosemary. And justice has been served.'

11

But it was not over, not yet, for I still didn't know why Cross had been so determined to kill me. As Will busied himself turning the carriage around and taking us back to the house I had mistakenly believed to be Rosehaven, I sat in silence, stunned by everything that had happened this night, by the deaths I had witnessed and how close I myself had come to dying. All at once I felt so drained, it was all I could do to keep my eyes open. I wanted to sleep, and in sleep, forget this entire sorry business.

Incredibly, I *did* doze off, for the next time I opened my eyes I saw that we were back at the house, and that the storm was finally passing.

Will hurried around the horse and helped me down. I went up the steps, puddled here and there with rain, and waited while he saw to the care of the poor, shivering horse. At last he joined me and we went inside.

We went directly upstairs to my suite, leaving a trail of rainwater behind us. The door was locked when I tried to enter, and I heard Jane call tremulously, 'Who's there? You'd better not try to enter, or I'll brain you!'

'Jane,' I said. 'It's me.'

I heard the key turn in the lock and then Jane was peering out into the hallway, her eyes wide with fear. In her left hand she held a poker.

'Mrs. Shaw!' she breathed, and sagged with relief. 'I heard all the commotion downstairs and well, we just didn't know what to do for the best . . . '

I went past her and said huskily, 'It . . . it's all right now. We're safe. We're . . . all safe.'

That was all Jonathan and Frances needed to hear. They came bolting out from where they had been hiding beneath the bed and into my waiting arms, both of them talking at once. As near as I could tell, they both wanted me to know that they had been really brave but worried about me, and that Jane had been the best protector they could have asked for. Jane herself set the poker aside somewhat sheepishly.

When the children were finished with me, they ran to Will and, heedless of the rain, he knelt and gathered them into his arms and hugged them back. After a moment, he stood up again and said softly, 'Thank you, Jane.'

She nodded an acknowledgement. 'Are we really safe?' she asked.

'Yes.'

'Safe from . . . what, exactly?'

'That,' I said, 'is a very good question.'

'And you deserve an answer, all of you,' said Will. 'But first of all, get out of those wet things and into something dry and warm, Rosemary. And Jane — get your things together. You're coming with us as well.'

'Where to, sir?' Jane asked uncertainly.

'To the man who can explain everything,' he said.

'My Uncle Joseph?' I hazarded.

He nodded and clapped his hands. 'Yes. Now, come on, hurry up! The sooner we all leave this Godforsaken place behind us, the better!'

I could only agree.

★ ★ ★

After making sure we were all safely in the Phaeton, Will climbed to the seat and drove us away from that house of intrigue. I didn't bother to look back. I had meant what I said. I never wanted to see that place again, and knew now that I never would.

The carriage took us around the bend in the drive and after a time we drove past the overturned Brougham and the awful, charred remains in the tobacco field.

In Phoenix Port, Will brought the

coach to a halt outside the village constable's cottage and rapped at the door. By now the hour was late, and it was a little while before the constable opened the door. He was wearing a nightshirt, his gray hair was sticking up and he did not look pleased to have been disturbed from his sleep. Will spoke to him in a low tone, once pointing back the way we had just come.

As he heard about the crash of the Brougham and the death of Hayden Cross in the tobacco field, the constable's eyes widened and he suddenly became alert. He began to question Will, but Will produced his wallet and opened it up for the constable's inspection. Whatever the constable saw there made him stand a little straighter and nod rapidly.

Will came back to the coach and soon the village fell behind us. In the coach itself, Jonathan and Frances had fallen asleep, nestled up against Jane, and she was happy to cuddle and comfort them as they dreamed.

The night was dark and cold and still smelled of rain. After a while I asked Will how far my uncle's house was. He smiled at me. 'The *real* Rosehaven, you mean?'

'Yes,' I said. 'The *real* Rosehaven.'

He tilted his head toward the road ahead. 'We're there,' he said.

Even by moonlight I could see that the house — the *real* Rosehaven — was magnificent . . . and quite, quite beautiful.

Will went on ahead of us and worked the bell-pull. As the rest of us climbed the steps, the door swung open and a maid appeared. She recognized Will immediately, and hurried back into the house, leaving Will himself to guide us inside. We crossed a wide foyer to a set of rich oak double doors, which the maid had opened for us.

'After you,' said Will, smiling.

Hesitantly, I went into the room ahead of the others. It was a cheerful sitting room, bright and colorful and a world away from the house where I had known such horror. An elderly man in a dark suit was standing in the center of the room, looking at me. He was perhaps seventy, with a long face and a large nose and a mouth that, just then, looked somewhat sober. He was bald but for the gray hair that still grew thick at his temples and above his ears, and his eyebrows were shaggy, and just a shade darker. His eyes were blue, and almost startling in their kindness and warmth.

'Rosemary?' he said.

Unable to speak, I nodded.

His lips moved then, and he smiled. His entire face transformed as he opened his arms and came forward. 'Welcome, child, welcome!'

And I *did* feel welcome — for the first time in so very long.

I stepped into his embrace and hugged him back, and after everything I had been through that evening, it felt wonderful. 'Uncle Joseph,' I said, and my voice cracked a little as I said it.

'Come,' he said. 'Mary — take our guests' coats, if you please! And hot drinks — I expect they're chilled to the bone!'

Then he saw the children and his eyes went wide.

'Ah, Master Jonathan and Mistress Frances, I do declare! Come here, children, and say hello to your Uncle Jo!'

The children were wary . . . until Uncle Joseph hurried to a corner, from which he produced two gaily-wrapped boxes. These immediately caught the children's' attention, and he handed one to each of them. 'I have no idea what could be inside them,' he said. 'But whatever it is . . . is for you!'

Children are nothing if not resilient. They both looked at me, and I nodded.

'Thank you,' said Jonathan.

'Thank you, Uncle Jo,' added Frances.

And then they were tearing the paper from their presents, and shortly thereafter Jonathan was examining a beautiful toy train set, while Frances was hugging a pretty doll as if it were already a beloved friend.

After Will introduced Jane, Uncle Joseph gestured that we should be seated. As he sat down, some of his good humor faded, and he looked at Will. 'It was, then, as we suspected?' he asked.

Will nodded. 'I'm afraid so, Mr. Trent.'

The older man seemed to deflate a little. 'And Hayden . . . ?'

'He's dead,' said Will. 'There was an accident. He was struck by lightning.'

The old man bowed his head for a few seconds. When he looked up again, I was surprised to see tears shining in his so-kind eyes.

'I expect you would like to know what this was all about?' he said, addressing me.

'I would.'

His sigh was heavy. 'You might find it hard to believe, but Hayden Cross was the best business partner a man could have wished for,' he said. 'He was astute, thorough, he had an ability to get things done and a streak of iron in him that I myself never possessed, and never *wished* to possess. But for all our many differences, we complemented each other. I believe that was why we enjoyed such success in our business endeavors.

'For all his faults, I liked him. But he could be a vain, self-centered man. He had a high opinion of himself and truly believed himself superior to others — sometimes, even to me. And yet there was one person with whom he felt truly comfortable — his wife, Elizabeth. When she died a few years ago, something in him, some small spark of charity that Elizabeth had kindled within him . . . that died, also. He was never the same man after that. He grew bitter and ever more ruthless. More than once I had to watch him, to make sure he didn't take his grief out on any of our employees, for that was the kind of man he became — cruel, heartless and vindictive.'

I cleared my throat. 'Excuse me,' I said softly, 'but what has all this to do with me?'

Uncle Joseph looked directly at me. 'Before Elizabeth came into his life,' he said, 'Hayden was an incorrigible womanizer. His need to take and possess any woman who took his fancy was almost akin to an obsession — perhaps *addiction* is a better term. All that stopped when he met Elizabeth, of course. She was a wonderful, wonderful influence upon him. But before she came into his life, he was almost insatiable in his desires.

'One such 'conquest' — a distasteful expression when used in this context — was a maid who used to work here. Her name was Catherine Palmer. Hayden seduced her, and left her heavy with child. The poor girl was beside herself — she was, after all, only seventeen, and she faced ruin if Hayden refused to marry her.'

'And he *did* refuse,' I guessed.

'Oh, yes. Marry a serving girl? That

was so far beneath Hayden that to him the very notion was laughable. He told her as much, and instructed her to leave my employ and never let him see her again.'

I thought about Cross's cold, ice-chip eyes, and could easily believe him capable of doing something so cruel.

'Catherine came to see me one day, and asked if she might be released from her position,' he went on. 'I was surprised — she had always seemed so happy in my employ. When I asked her if anything was wrong, she said there was nothing. But to her credit, she was a poor liar, and when pressed, she finally broke down and confessed what had happened.

'I knew at once that I could not allow her to face her uncertain future without help. So, to keep her parents from discovering what had happened, I told her that I would send her to a property of mine in New Brunswick, ostensibly to oversee some restorations I was having done there . . . but in reality to give her enough time to have her baby, and then decide whether or not she wanted to keep it.

'The ruse was successful. No one here ever discovered her secret.

'But when she returned here, her spirit had been broken by Hayden's harsh treatment, and her own misplaced shame. All she wanted to do was start life afresh in a different part of the country. As difficult as that was, she knew it would be twice as hard if she had to support a baby as well as herself.'

'So she decided to give up the baby?' My voice was a near-whisper now.

He nodded.

'I could not allow the child to go to an orphanage,' he said, and now his voice was thick with emotion. 'From the moment I saw it, I knew it was special, and I loved it for its specialness. I have no idea how I knew it, but know it I *did* — that the child inherited everything that was pure and good from its mother, and none of the darkness of its father.' He looked at me very steadily now. 'So I asked my sister if she would take the child and raise it as her own.'

The room was silent but for the children, playing happily with their toys.

'*You* were that baby, Rosemary,' he said.

I must have swayed a little, because Will hurriedly placed an arm around my shoulders to support me.

Everything I had believed to this point was suddenly overturned. I was born out of wedlock. My mother was not really my mother, my father was not really my father. My real mother was a poor young girl whose life had been ruined by Hayden Cross . . . and most shocking of all, that Hayden Cross was my real father.

I felt sick.

I remembered the strange way he had looked at me the first time he saw me, and now I understood why. He was looking at his daughter! And the way he had hesitated when referring to my children — his *grandchildren!*

What had he really been thinking when he saw us? I wished it could have been pride and love and joy, but it had been none of those things. He had been absolutely devoid of any emotion whatsoever . . . except hatred.

'Is that why he wanted me dead?' I asked in a small voice.

Uncle Joseph shook his head. 'I recently had an illness,' he replied. 'In itself it was nothing particularly serious, but it did make me think about my future, what's left of it. I had always felt somewhat guilty that I lost contact with my — *our* — family, Rosemary. I was young and ambitious and after a time the business kept me so busy that I just . . . drifted away from them. The longer it went on, the harder it became to renew contact, and for that I shall always be sorry.

'But I had realized long ago that there might still be a way I could make amends, after a fashion. And so I decided to call this place Rosehaven and hold it towards your future.'

For the first time, then, I recognized the significance in the name. This house, it was meant to be a haven . . . for Rosemary!

'I have followed your life all these years, Rosemary, albeit from a distance,' he went on. 'And I was so sad to learn that your husband had died. But that settled the matter for me. I decided to invite you to live here for as long as you desire, to settle your husband's debts, and to make provision to keep you and your children safe and financially sound for the rest of your lives. I only made one mistake — I told Hayden of my intention.

'He was furious. He felt that I was giving in to some sickly sense of obligation where no obligation existed. He hated the idea that one day, my share of our business might fall to you, his illegitimate daughter. As far as Hayden was concerned, we would *both* leave our share of the business to his distant relative, a nephew named David.

'We argued bitterly about it. And after he left here that last time, I suspected that he was just angry and callous enough to do something to prevent me from going ahead with my plan. That's when I hired Mr. Hennessey, here.'

I looked at Will. He said, 'I'm an operative from the Pinkerton Detective Agency in Chicago. Your uncle instructed me to keep an eye on you, and it was as well that he did. I assume you sent a letter to your uncle, confirming that you would be coming to live with him?'

'Yes, of course.'

'I never received it,' said Uncle Joseph. 'I suspect that Hayden paid someone on my staff to intercept it and deliver it to him, instead.'

'That much was plain when you arrived in Phoenix Port,' Will continued. 'I had been watching the station for your arrival for some time. When you *did* arrive, a man I didn't recognize took you to a house that I later discovered Hayden Cross had rented. I kept the place under observation — '

I suddenly remembered that stormy night when I had looked out onto the gardens and seen a muffled figure quickly vanishing back into the woods. 'That was you!'

'It was indeed,' he confessed. 'And I was following you when you almost fainted, the day the children started school.

'That was the turning point. Based upon what you told me that day, I began to understand Cross's entire deception. He told you that your uncle no longer wanted you at Rosehaven, and expected you to return to Connecticut the following day, never to be heard from again. When you elected to stay, that presented him with a dilemma. There was no way that your uncle would somehow 'return home' and tell you to your face that you were no longer wanted there — as you now know, he was ignorant of the entire scheme! And so, all that remained was . . . '

He stopped abruptly.

I said, 'Murder.'

He nodded. 'I am so sorry, Rosemary. You asked for none of this, and yet you had to suffer through *all* of it. The only consolation is that your real mother gave you up for the best of reasons, because she cared for you and knew she would never be able to look after you the way you deserved to be looked after. And as for the people you always believed to be your real parents — '

'As far as I'm concerned, they *were* my real parents,' I said. 'No parents could have treated me better, and I will love them forever.'

'I'm glad to hear you say that,' he replied. 'Because that's what you've finally found — a home filled with love.'

He looked deep into my eyes when he said that word, and I knew that my illegitimacy made no difference to him at all.

'Now,' said Uncle Joseph, 'as hard as it is to do so, I want you to put all of this behind you. And I promise you, from the bottom of my heart, that you are safe now . . . and never was a guest more welcome. You, the children . . . and of course, you, young lady!' He smiled at Jane. 'You have a job here for as long as you want it. And for protecting Jonathan and Frances so well, I doubt you will find a more generous employer anywhere!'

'Thank you, sir,' Jane said shyly.

'What about this . . . David?' I asked 'Cross's nephew? He will have something to say about all this, I'm sure.'

'Don't you worry about David,' Uncle Joseph replied. 'He has not the slightest interest in running a business. He lives in New York, where he studies art. And though he will doubtless be sorry to hear of the death of an uncle he barely knew, there was precious little love lost between them. I suspect he will soon get over the loss — provided we continue to send him his rather generous monthly allowance . . . which we will. He will doubtless also inherit Hayden's half of the business, but he will probably be glad to sell it to the first buyer who comes along — me.'

I considered everything I had learned, and finally said, 'Thank you, Uncle Jo. You have been more than generous. And though I don't wish to seem ungrateful, I'm afraid I cannot accept your invitation, after all.'

His expression slackened. 'What? I . . . I don't understand.'

'Will said something to me earlier, something I didn't really understand at the time. He told me that I had no idea then what lay in my future, except that it might be something so grand that there would be no room in it for him.' I looked at Will. 'You would never come to call again, would you, Will? For fear that folk might think you were only after me because of my position here, as the mistress of Rosehaven.'

He nodded sadly. 'You have financial security now, Rosemary,' he said. 'And you can set your sights a little higher than a humble, footloose detective.'

'And if I don't want that?' I replied. 'No, Will. If it means losing you, I would happily reject everything my uncle has offered me.'

Uncle Jo stood up. 'Oh, for heaven's sake,' he said, 'there must be a way we can settle this silliness!'

'I wish there were, sir,' said Will. 'I'll be honest with you, I had no expectation that I would fall in love when the Agency sent me out here, but fall in love I did. In Rosemary I found the person I want to settle down with, and in her children, I made two fine little friends whose minds are as open and questing as my own. I could wish for no other companions with whom to share the remainder of my days. But I have to face facts. Rosemary has a new life now, whether she cares for it or not. I will not take that away from her.'

'Young people!' Uncle Jo lamented.

'All right — Rosemary, I promised you a home here. And I promised that I would clear John's debts so that you may start afresh. Will you at least take the money — no more, no less — even if it leaves you as poor as a church mouse, once those debts are paid?'

I felt the tears in my eyes. 'If it means I can convince Will to stay.'

'Then that is what we shall do,' said Uncle Jo, clapping his hands. 'You will get not a penny more than you need, my girl! And because of that, no one will ever be able to accuse you of romancing Rosemary here for her vast fortune, young Will . . . because there won't be one!'

I felt Will's eyes on me. There was such deep love in them, so much warmth and desire — all the things I had been deprived of during my time with John. I loved John still — he was, after all, the father of my children, and he had never been a bad man, only one preoccupied with matters of business. But as I looked back at Will, I knew for certain that I loved him too, in a completely different way. Here was a man who would always put my children and I first, and be content to do so. A good man.

I held out my hand and he took it.

'And in due course,' said Uncle Jo, 'we will have to start thinking about the wedding . . . once a suitable period of mourning has been observed, of course. And if you would allow me to, I would consider it a privilege to give you a sizeable parcel of land from this very estate upon which you may build your own home. That way the name Rosehaven will still have relevance . . . and you, my dear girl, will still be its mistress.'

It was the perfect solution. And I am delighted to tell you, dear reader, that that was the way everything turned out.

We do hope that you have enjoyed reading this large print book.

Did you know that all of our titles are available for purchase?

We publish a wide range of high quality large print books including:
Romances, Mysteries, Classics
General Fiction
Non Fiction and Westerns

Special interest titles available in large print are:
The Little Oxford Dictionary
Music Book, Song Book
Hymn Book, Service Book

Also available from us courtesy of Oxford University Press:
Young Readers' Dictionary
(large print edition)
Young Readers' Thesaurus
(large print edition)

For further information or a free brochure, please contact us at:
Ulverscroft Large Print Books Ltd.,
The Green, Bradgate Road, Anstey,
Leicester, LE7 7FU, England.
Tel: (00 44) **0116 236 4325**
Fax: (00 44) **0116 234 0205**

WISHES CAN COME TRUE

Angela Britnell

Meg Harper is shocked when the man she knows as Lucca Raffaele, who stood her up in Italy the previous summer, arrives to stay at her family home in Tennessee — this time calling himself her step-cousin, Jago Merryn ... Jago is there to acquire a local barbecue business, but discovering the woman who came close to winning his heart is only one of the surprises in store for him. Can they move past their mistrust and seize a second chance for their wishes to come true?